Moldy Strawberries

STORIES BY CAIO FERNANDO ABREU

Translated from the Portuguese
by Bruna Dantas Lobato

archipelago books

Library of Congress Cataloging-in-Publication Data available upon request

Archipelago Books
232 3rd Street #A111
Brooklyn, NY 11215
www.archipelagobooks.org

Distributed by Penguin Random House
www.penguinrandomhouse.com

Cover art: Jean Dubuffet, *Evolving Portrait* (1952) The Museum of Modern Art,
New York © 2022 Artists Rights Society (ARS), New York / ADAGP, Paris

This work is made possible by the New York State Council on the Arts with
the support of the Office of the Governor and the New York State Legislature.
Funding for the translation of this book was provided by a grant from
the Carl Lesnor Family Foundation.

This publication was made possible with support from Lannan
Foundation, the Nimick Forbesway Foundation, the National Endowment for
the Arts, and the New York City Department of Cultural Affairs.

PRINTED IN THE UNITED STATES

MOLDY STRAWBERRIES

Moldy

Dejadme en este campo, llorando.

—Federico García Lorca, "¡Ay!"

The fire and smoke monster
stole my white clothes.
The air is dirty
and the season is new.
    —Henrique do Valle, "Monstro de fumaça" ["Smoke Monster"]

Contents

In memory of
John Lennon
Elis Regina
Henrique do Valle
Rômulo Coutinho de Azevedo
and all my dead friends

To Caetano Veloso.
And for
Maria Clara Jorge (Cacaia)
Sonia Maria Barbosa (Sonia de Oxum Apará)
and all my living friends

As for writing, a living dog is worth much more.
— Clarice Lispector, *The Hour of the Star*

I thought it was lovely, back then, hearing a poet say that he writes for the same reason that trees bear fruit. Only much later did I come to realize this was all but affectation: that men are intrinsically different from trees and need to know the purpose of their fruits, choosing what they'll bear, studying who will receive them, and not always giving them the ripe ones, but the rotten, and even the poisoned.
— Osman Lins, *Guerra sem testemunhas* [*Unwitnessed War*]

Dialogue

For Luiz Arthur Nunes

A: You're my friend.

B: Huh?

A: You're my friend, I said.

B: What?

A: I said you're my friend.

B: What are you trying to say?

A: I'm just saying you're my friend, my *companheiro*. That's all.

B: There's something behind this, I can tell.

A: No. There's nothing. Don't be so paranoid.

B: That's not what I'm talking about.

A: What are you talking about, then?

B: I'm talking about what you said, just now.

A: Oh, right. That I'm your friend.

B: No, that's not how it went: that I'm your friend.

A: You feel it too?

B: What?

[13]

A: That you're my friend?

B: Stop confusing me. There's something behind this, I know it.

A: Behind the friend?

B: Yeah.

A: Nope.

B: Don't you feel it?

A: That you're my friend? I do, yes. Of course I do. Don't you?

B: It's not that, but not like this.

A: You don't want it to be like this?

B: It's not that I don't want it: it's that it's not.

A: Stop confusing me, please, just stop confusing me. It was clear in the beginning.

B: And now it's not?

A: Now it is. Do you want to?

B: What?

A: Be my friend.

B: Be your friend?

A: Yeah.

B: Friend – *companheiro*?

A: Yes.

B: I don't know. Please, stop confusing me. It was clear in the beginning. There's something behind this, don't you see?

A: I see it. I want it.

B: Want what?

A: For you to be my friend.

B: Huh?

A: I want you to be my friend, I said.

B: What?

A: I said I want you to be my friend.

B: You said that?

A: I said that?

B: No, that's not how it went: I said that.

A: What?

B: That you're my friend.

A: Huh?

(ad infinitum)

The Survivors

For Jane Araújo, a Magra
(To be read to the soundtrack of Angela Ro Ro)

What about Sri Lanka? she asks me, dark and fierce, and I answer,
Why not? Undeterred, she continues: At least you could send me
postcards from there, so people would think wow, how did he end
up in Sri Lanka, what a crazy guy that one, huh, and they'd die of
saudade, isn't that what you care about? A kind of *saudade*: and you
in Sri Lanka, pretending to be Rimbaud, who never actually went
that far, so everyone would weep, oh how sweet he was and we
never offered him enough to make him stay with us, palm trees and
pineapples. Talking incessantly, she fans herself with an Angela Ro
Ro record while she smokes incessantly and drinks incessantly her
cheap vodka, no ice, no lime. As for me, her voice so hoarse, I'll
stick around and protest, spray paint against the nuclear plants, still
hungover, a monk day, a slut day, a Joplin day, a Mother Teresa day,
a shit day, while I keep that stupid eight-hour job to pay for that
authentic leather chair where your royal highness has parked your

precious ass, and this exotic Indian redwood coffee table where I'm resting my feet, bare and tired again, at the end of another week of useless battles, escapist fantasies, weak orgasms, late payments. But we've tried everything, I say, and she says, Yes, of cooooooourse, we've tried everything, even fucking, because after so many borrowed books, so many films seen together, so many sociopolitical existential blahblah shared points of view, it could only lead to this: the bed. We really tried, but it was a bust. What happened, what in the name of God happened, I kept thinking afterwards as I lit a cigarette with another, and I didn't want to think about it but I couldn't get it out of my mind and your limp dick and my nipples which didn't even get hard, for the first time ever, you told me, and I believed you, for the first time ever, I told you, but I don't know if you believed me as well. I want to say yes, that I believed her, but she doesn't stop, so much mental spiritual moral existential attraction and none of it physical, I didn't want to accept that was all it was: that we were different, oh we were so different, we were better, we were more, we were superior, we were chosen, we were vaguely sacred but in the end my nipples wouldn't get hard and your dick didn't go up. Too much culture kills people's bodies, man, too many films, too many books, too many words, I could only consume you by masturbating, there was the entire Library of Alexandria keeping our bodies apart, I stuck my finger up my pussy night after night saying deeper, sweetheart, burst with me, fuck me, then I'd flip over onto my stomach and cry on my pillow because back then there was still all this guilt disgust shame, but now it's fine, *The Hite Report* liberated fucking. Not that it was too little love, quite the opposite, you told me later, it was too much of it, did you really believe that? In that filthy bar where we used to drown our impotence with buckets of idiotic juvenile lyricism, and I said no, dear, it's just that being the bored-bourgeois-good-intellectuals that we are, your thing is men and my thing is women, we could even make a great couple, like Virginia Woolf and her lover, what was her name again? Vita, right, Vita Sackville-West and her fag husband, now calm down, darling, I have nothing against fags, would you pass me the vodka, what? And do I look like I have money for Wyborowa? No, I don't have anything against lesbians, I don't have anything against degenerates in general, I don't have anything against whatever sounds like: an attempt. I ask for a cigarette and she tosses the pack at my face like she's throwing a brick, I've been getting anxious, my friend, dear old word that one, anxiety, two decades of everyday life but I get, I get, I have something tight here in my chest, a tussle, a thirst, a heaviness, oh don't start with these stories of we-betray-all-our-ideals, I've never had any fucking ideals of any kind, I just wanted to save what's mine, what an egocentric elitist capitalist thing to do, I just wanted to be happy, dumb, fat, ignorant, and totally happy, man. It could have worked out between us, or not, I don't even know what that means, but back then we hadn't figured out yet that you wanted to take it up the ass and I wanted to lick pussy, oh how adorable our books by

Marx, then Marcuse, then Reich, then Castañeda, then Laing under the arm, all the foolish colonized dreams in our little idiotic heads, scholarship at the Sorbonne, tea with Simone and Jean-Paul in Paris in the '50s, then the '60s in London listening to *here comes the sun here comes the sun, little darling*, then the '70s in New York dancing disco at Studio 54, now in the '80s we're here, chewing on this nasty thing and unable to swallow or spit it out or even to forget the sour taste in our mouths. I've read everything, man, I've tried macrobiotics psychoanalysis drugs acupuncture suicide yoga dance swimming jogging astrology roller-skating Marxism Candomblé gay clubs ecology, all that's left is this knot in my chest, so now what do I do? I'm not copying Pessoa but in each corner of my room there's an image of Buddha, a picture of Oshun, another of baby Jesus, a poster of Freud, sometimes I light a candle, pray, burn incense, smudge sage, ward off the evil eye with salt in every corner, I'm not asking you for a solution, you'll get to enjoy the people of Sri Lanka and later will send me a postcard telling me whatever, a night like last night, by the river, there must be some river over there, a murky river, full of dark reeds, but yesterday by the river, without making any plans, suddenly, completely by chance, I saw a guy with olive skin and slanted eyes who was... Huh? Of course there's some dignity to all of this, the question is where, not in this dark city, not on this poor, putrid planet, inside me? Now, don't start with self-knowledge-redeemers again, I already know everything about myself, I've dropped acid more than fifty times, I've done six years of psychoanalysis, I got sick of clinics, remember? You'd bring me Argentine apples and Italian photo comics, Rossana Galli, Franco Andrei, Michela Roc, Sandro Moretti, and I'd look at you full of Mandrax and drool sob I lost my joy, my night fell, they stole my hope, while you, generous and positive, touched my shoulder with your hand and in spite of everything lively saying over and over, react, *companheira*, react, the precise motivation behind your little privileged head, your creative po-ten-tial, your left-libertarian lucidity, blahblahblah. People turned into corpses decomposing in front of me, my skin was sad and dirty, the nights never ended, no one touched me, but I reacted, got unsick, went back to what they say is normal, and where's the motivation, where's the fight, where's the creative po-ten-tial? Do I kill, not kill, quench my thirst with dykes at Ferro's Bar, or get drunk alone on a Saturday as I wait for the phone to ring, and it never rings, in this apartment I can only afford with the sweat of the creative po-ten-tial I pull out of my ass, for eight hours each day for that fucked-up multinational. But, I try to say, and she cuts me off, gently, Of course it's not your fault, love, we fell into the exact same mousetrap, the only difference is that you think you can escape, and I want to wallow in the pain of the metal stuck deep in my dry throat, pass me the cigarette, no, I'm not desperate, not more than I've always been, *nothing special, baby*, I'm not drunk or crazy, I'm lucid as fuck and I confidently know I don't have a way out, don't worry too much, dear, after you leave I'll have a cold shower, some warm milk with eucalyptus honey, ginseng, and Bromazepam, then I'll lie down, then go to sleep, then I'll wake up and live for a week on sencha and brown rice, absolutely saintly, absolutely pure, absolutely clean, then I'll have all the drinks, I'll snort five grams, crash my car into a wall or call the suicide hotline at four in the morning or pester some fool while whimpering things like I-need-a-reason-to-live-so-much-and-I-know-this-reason-is-only-inside-me-blahblahblah-blahblahblah, until the sun comes up behind the dark buildings, but don't worry, I won't take any drastic measures, beyond keeping going, is there anything more self-destructive than persisting without faith? Pat me gently on my head, on my heart, she stops and asks, I had so much love once, I need it so much, so much, man, I haven't been allowed. I stretch out my arms and she's suddenly so small pressed against my chest, asking me if she's really ugly and sort of slutty and too old and totally drunk, I didn't use to have these lines around my eyes, I didn't use to have these creases around my mouth, I didn't use to look like such a tired dyke, and I tell her again that no, that she looks great like that, disheveled and alive, she asks me to put on some music and I choose Chopin's Nocturne in E-flat major, No. 2, I want to leave her like this, sleeping in the dark on this old couch, next to the wilted poppies, absorbed in the distant lullaby from the piano, but she tenses up, violently, asks me to play Angela Ro Ro again, so I flip the record over, my love my great love, we dizzily walk to the bathroom together, where I hold her head over the toilet while she throws up, and without meaning to I throw up too, at the same time, the two of us in an embrace, sour particles over our tongues when our mouths meet, but she flushes the toilet and pushes me toward the living room, toward the door, asking me to go, and kicks me out to the hallway saying, Don't forget to send me that postcard from Sri Lanka, that murky river, that olive skin, may something very beautiful happen to you, I wish you a lot of faith, in anything, it doesn't matter what, like that faith we once had, wish me something very beautiful too, anything wonderful, anything that makes me believe in anything again, that makes us believe in everyone again, that takes away this rotten taste of failure from my mouth, of defeat with no grandeur, there's no way, *companheiro*, we got lost in the middle of the road and we never had a map, no one gives rides anymore and night is about to fall. The lock turns in the door. I need to lean against the wall so I won't fall. Behind the wood of the door, mixed with the piano and Angela's hoarse voice, I can hear her say over and over that everything's fine, everything is going along fine, just fine, fine. *Axé, axé, axé*, I repeat until the elevator arrives, *axé, axé, axé, odara!*

The Day Uranus Entered Scorpio
(Old Story with Benefits)

*For Zé and Lygia Sávio Teixeira
and for Lucrécia (Luc Ziz or Cesar Esposito)*

They were all relaxed at home when the guy in the red shirt suddenly stormed in and announced that Uranus was entering Scorpio. The three of them stopped what they were doing and stared at him without saying anything. Maybe they didn't understand what he said, or they didn't care to. Or they simply weren't willing to interrupt their reading, leave their spot at the window, or stop eating their chicken thighs, to pay attention to anything else, especially to something like Uranus entering Scorpio, Jupiter leaving Aquarius, or the moon being void of course.

It was Saturday night, almost summer, and there were so many concerts and plays and full bars and parties and movie premieres at midnight and people meeting and motorcycles zooming by around the city, and it was so hard to give all that up to stay in the apartment reading, watching other people's joy through the window, or trying to find some sliver of meat on the bones of the cold chicken left over from lunch. As they'd given up their Saturday, the three of them sitting there quietly listening to old Pink Floyd albums, so the neighbors wouldn't complain like last time and then the police would come and the landlord would threaten to shut down that drug den (they didn't like the expression, but that was what the neighbors, landlord, and police called it, tossing their secondhand books and Indian cushions everywhere, like they expected to find something illicit under them) – thus having given up their Saturday, and tacitly restored the peace with the low volume and almost no curiosity about each other, since they'd known each other for so long, they didn't want to be thrown out of this peace that was so wisely and modestly earned, since the night before had revealed empty pockets and wallets. So they vaguely looked at the guy in the red shirt standing in the middle of their living room. And said nothing.

The guy who'd left his spot by the window made like he was paying close attention to the music, and said that he really liked that bit with the organ and the violins, that it sounded like a *medieval cavalryman*. The guy in the red shirt understood he was trying to change the subject, and asked if by any chance he'd ever seen a medieval cavalryman. He said no, but with the organ and all those violins in the background, he pictured an armored warrior on a white horse, riding into the wind, all very Knights of the Round Table, the outline of a castle on top of a distant hill – and the warrior was *medieval*, he stressed, he was sure of that. He was going to keep describing this scene, he was thinking of adding some pine trees, twilight, maybe a crescent moon, perhaps even a lake, when the woman who'd been reading a book lowered her glasses again, which she'd raised up to her forehead when the guy in the red shirt came in, and read a passage from Ernest Becker's *The Denial of Death*:

> *Men are so necessarily mad that not to be mad would amount to another form of madness.* Necessarily *because the existential dualism makes an impossible situation, an excruciating dilemma.* Mad *because, as we shall see, everything that man does in his symbolic world is an attempt to deny and overcome his grotesque fate. He literally drives himself into a blind obliviousness with social games, psychological tricks, personal preoccupations so far removed from the reality of his situation that they are forms of madness – agreed madness, shared madness, disguised and dignified madness, but madness all the same.*

When she finished reading and looked around the room with delight, the guy who'd left the window returned to his spot, and the guy in the red shirt remained still and slightly out of breath in the middle of the room, while the other one stared at the bare bone of a chicken thigh. He then said he didn't really like thighs as much anymore, that he preferred the neck, at his house growing up everyone always fought, because he had three siblings and they all liked the thighs, except for Valéria, who found chickens disgusting; later, as a teenager, he preferred the breast, he spent five or six years eating nothing but the breast, and now he loved the neck. The others looked a little shocked hearing this, and he explained that the neck actually had many secret pleasures, exactly like that, very slowly, se-cret pleas-ures, and in that moment the record came to an end and his words echoed a bit provocatively in the silent air while he continued to stare at the dry bone.

The guy in the red shirt took advantage of the silence to scream very loudly that Uranus was entering Scorpio. The others seemed disturbed, less so by the information and more by the noise, and said *shh*, that he should lower his voice, didn't he remember what happened last time? He said the last time didn't matter, that *now* Uranus was entering Scorpio. *To-day*, he said slowly, eyes shining. It had been there for some five years, he added, and the others asked at the same time, *what-had-been-where*? *Uranus*, the guy in the red shirt explained, in my eighth House, the House of Death, didn't you know I could be dying right now? and he almost looked relieved, if it weren't for all the restlessness. The others exchanged looks and the woman holding the book started to tell a very long and convoluted story about a boy who suffered from schizophrenia who'd started *just* like this, he took an interest in things like alchemy, astrology, chiromancy, numerology, things he'd read god-knows-where (he read a lot, and when he told a story, he never knew for certain where he'd first read it, sometimes he couldn't even be sure if he'd lived it or read it). He ended up committed, she said, that's how many schizoid processes go. He looked directly at her as she said *schizoid processes*, the other two seemed very impressed, it was hard to say if it was because they respected the woman and thought her very refined, or if it was simply because they wanted to scare the guy in the red shirt. At any rate, they were left with a silence full of sharp angles until one of them moved from his place by the window to turn the record over. And when the bubbles of sound started to burst in the middle of the room, they all looked relieved and almost happy again.

Then the guy in the red shirt took out of his bag a book that looked like he'd bound it himself, and asked if anyone spoke French. One of them threw the chicken bone into the ashtray, as if to violently say that he didn't, and he looked at the man by the window, who wasn't by the window anymore but on the rug, browsing their record collection. He suddenly stopped and looked at the woman, who hesitated for a moment before saying that she spoke a little, and everyone seemed a bit disappointed. The guy in the red shirt quietly said that it was all right, and started to read from André Barbault's *Astrologie*:

> *La position de cet astre en secteur situe le lieu ou l'être dégage au maximum son individualité dans une voie de supersonnalisation, à la faveur d'un développement d'énergie ou d'une croissance exagerée qui est moins une abondance de force de vie qu'une tension particulière d'enérgie. Ici, l'être tend à affirmer une volonté lucide d'independance qui peut le conduire à une expression supérieure et originale de sa personalité. Dans la dissonance, son exigence conduit à l'insensibilité, à la dureté, à l'excessif, à l'extrémisme, au jusqu'au'boutisme, à l'aventure, aux bouleversements.*

He finished reading and slowly looked at the three of them, one by one, but only the woman smiled, saying that she didn't know the word *bouleversements*. One of the men remembered that *boulevard* means *street*, and that therefore it must mean something related to a street, to walking in the streets a lot. They kept guessing, one of them looking for a dictionary, the guy in the red shirt looking from one to the other without saying anything. After all the books had been combed through and the dictionary was nowhere to be found and the other side of the record also came to an end, he read the passage again very slowly, emphasizing each syllable with a pronunciation the others admired, though they didn't say anything:

L'être tend à affirmer une volonté lucide d'independence qui peut le conduire à une expression supérieure et originale de sa personalité.

Then he asked if the others understood it, and they said they did, it sounded very similar to Portuguese, *lucide*, for example, and *originale*, were incredibly easy. But they didn't seem like they understood. His eyes shone again, he looked like he was about to cry when suddenly, unexpectedly, he jumped toward the window and yelled that he'd jump, that no one understood him, that nothing was worthwhile anymore, that he was so sick of everything he wouldn't even bet his own shit on the future.

The guy in the red shirt went as far as putting one leg over the windowsill, opening his arms, but the other two men grabbed him in time and took him to the bedroom, asking very gently what had just happened, repeating that he was too nervous, that everything was fine, just fine. The woman with the glasses held his hand and stroked his hair while he cried, one of the men said he'd go to the kitchen to make some mugwort or chamomile tea, the woman said that lemon balm was good for times like this, and the other said he'd put on that Indian music he liked so much, though everyone else hated it, except he'd have to turn the volume all the way up so they could hear it from the bedroom. The tea came soon after, hot and good, and they appeared with a joint as well, which they smoked together, one at a time, and things slowly became more harmonious and calm, until someone knocked on the door with such force it sounded more like kicking than knocking.

It was the landlord, yelling at them to lower the volume and repeating those same unpleasant things. The woman with the glasses said she was very sorry, but unfortunately that night they couldn't keep the volume down, it wasn't a night like the others, it was very special, she was very sorry. She took off her glasses and asked if the landlord knew that Uranus was entering Scorpio.

Back in the bedroom, the guy in the red shirt heard this and smiled a big smile before falling asleep with the others holding hands. Then he dreamt he was gently gliding over a golden and luminous surface as if on a pair of skates. He didn't know if it was a ring of Saturn or a moon of Jupiter. Perhaps Titan.

Passing through a Great Sorrow

For Paula Dip
(To be read to the soundtrack of Erik Satie)

The first time the telephone rang, he didn't move. He sat there on the old, yellow cushion, covered with faded shepherdesses holding flower wreaths. The colorful, flickering lights from the muted TV made the room quiver, pale under the morbid and luxurious burgundy glow of some old movie. When the phone rang again, he was trying to remember if the name of the slow, scratchy melody coming from the other room was "Pleasant Despair" or "For a Pleasant Despair." Either way, he thought: despair. And pleasant.

The light from the streetlamp filtered in through the lace of the curtains, bluish, mixing with the washed-out color of the film. Before the phone rang a third time, he decided to get up – to check the name of the piece, he told himself, then headed to the other room, through the narrow hallway where his pants brushed against the striated leaf of a plant, as they always did. I need to find a new place for it, he thought, as he always did. And before reaching for the phone on the bookcase, he bent down over the records scattered across the floor, between an overflowing ashtray and a ceramic mug, nearly empty except for some residue at the bottom that formed a green paste, moist and dense. "*Désespoir Agréable*," he confirmed. Standing there, he grabbed the white sleeve and put it on the table while repeating in his head: either way, despair. And pleasant.

"Lui?" The familiar voice. "Hello? Is that you, Lui?"

"Here," he said.

"What are you up to?"

He sat down. Then he stretched out his arm and stared at his own palm. The spots flaking off, uric acid, they'd told him, slowly eating away at the skin.

"Hello? Can you hear me?"

"Hey," he said.

"I asked what you were doing."

"What I'm doing? Nothing. Just listening to music, watching TV." He relaxed his hand. "I was about to make some coffee. And go to sleep."

"Hello? Can you speak up?"

"But I'm not sure I have any left."

"What?"

"Nothing, it's not important. And you?"

On the other end of the line, she sighed. There was a brief silence, and then a dry click and a sort of puffing. She must've lit a cigarette, he thought. He mechanically leaned to the left to reach the ashtray full of cigarette butts and pulled it closer to the phone.

"What's going on?" he asked slowly, looking around for a pack of cigarettes.

"Listen. Don't you feel like taking a little walk?"

"I'm tired. Not really in the mood. And I have to get up early tomorrow."

"I'll come pick you up. Then I'll drop you off. We won't be long at all. We could go to a bar, to a movie theater, to a…"

"It's after ten," he said.

Her voice got a bit shrill.

"Then come to me. You don't want that either, do you? I have this great vodka. The best. You'll love it, haven't even opened it yet. Only thing missing is the lime. Will you bring one?" Her voice was suddenly so shrill he had to hold the phone away from his ear. For a moment, he just listened to the distant melody of a piano, slow and scratchy. Through the glass-door panes, with the light shining out back, he could see the tops of the green plants in the garden, scattered yellow leaves on the ground. Unconsciously, he almost shivered in the chill air. Or from a kind of fear. He rubbed the dry palm of his left hand against his thigh. Her voice sounded normal again. "And what if I went over there?"

His fingers brushed against the pack of cigarettes in his back pocket. He held the phone pressed between his shoulder and his face as he slowly pulled out the pack.

"It's just," he said.

"Lui?"

He held one of the cigarettes between his teeth. He bit it, softly.

"Hello? Lui? Are you there?"

He lit the cigarette, holding the phone even tighter against his shoulder, and he almost dropped the receiver. He took a deep drag. Then grabbed the phone again and slowly relaxed his sore shoulder as he exhaled the smoke.

"I was about to go to bed."

"What's this music in the background?" she suddenly asked.

He pulled the ashtray closer, then turned the record cover in his hands.

"It's called 'For a Pleasant Despair,'" he lied. "Do you like it?"

"I don't know. It makes me a little sleepy. Who is it?"

He tapped his cigarette on the rim of the ashtray three times, but no ashes fell off.

"Some guy. A lunatic."

"What's his name?"

"Erik Satie," he said softly. She didn't hear it.

"Lui? Hello? Lui?"

"Yeah."

"Am I pissing you off?" Again, he heard the brief silence, the dry click, the soft puffing. She must have lit another cigarette, he thought.

"No," he said.

"Am I annoying you? Tell me. I know I am."

"It's fine. I wasn't really doing anything."

"I can't sleep," she said, faintly.

"Are you already in bed?"

"Yeah. Reading. Then I felt like talking to you."

He took a deep drag. While he exhaled the smoke, he bent down again to pick up the ceramic mug. He dragged his finger against the bottom then nibbled on the small leaves with his front teeth.

"What were you reading?" he asked.

"Nothing. Some article in a magazine. Something about monocultures and sprays."

"What?"

"Huh?"

"What was it about?"

She coughed, then seemed to cheer up a bit.

"Stuff like that. Ecologies. Apparently if you keep growing the same thing in the soil for many years, it'll end up dying. The soil, not the thing, of course. Soy, for example. And eucalyptus too, it seems. It destroys the organic matter. Then slowly it all becomes desert. The soil is covered with isolated dots, empty. Deserted. Scattered all over the planet.

The record stopped, but he didn't move. After a moment, it started over again.

"Like when you spill drops of ink on a piece of paper. They spread, more and more. They end up meeting each other, you know? The desert gets bigger. Each time bigger. Deserts never stop growing, did you know that?"

"I did," he said.

"Horrible, isn't it?"

"And the sprays?"

"What?"

"The sprays. What's wrong with the sprays?"

"Oh, yeah. I saw it in the same magazine. It said that each time you spray deodorant – not just deodorant, anything, you know – it creates this thing. Oh, how can I say it? A hole, you know what I mean? A leak, a hole in the layer? What's it called?"

"The ozone layer," he said.

"Right, the ozone layer. The air we breathe, you know? The biosphere."

"It must look like a sieve by now, then," he said.

"What?"

"It must look like a sieve," he repeated slowly. "The layer. The biosphere. The ozone."

"Can you imagine, how horrible. Did you know that? Hello, Lui? Are you there?"

"I am."

"I think I got kind of horrified," she said. "And scared. Aren't you scared, Lui?"

"I'm tired."

On the other end of the line, she laughed. From the sound, he guessed that she laughed without really opening her mouth, just shaking her shoulders, shaking her head from side to side, a strand of hair falling over her eyes.

"Am I keeping you?" she asked. "You always say I'm keeping you. Like you're some property I saw and liked, a house. If I were a house I'd be one with a pool in the back. A huge garden. And air conditioning. What kind of house would you like to be, Lui?"

"I wouldn't want to be a house."

"What?"

"I'd like to be an apartment."

"All right, but what kind?"

He sighed.

"A studio. With no phone."

"What? Hello, Lui? Were you really not planning on doing anything?"

"Tea. I was about to make myself some tea."

"Wasn't it coffee? I thought you said you were going to make coffee."

"There's no powder left." He shook the ashtray full of cigarette butts. Some specks of ash fell out on the white cover of the record with the abstract drawing in the middle. Carefully, he collected them in a pile over the purple corner of the main picture. "No filters either. And I just remembered I have this amazing tea. It even came with a crazy list of uses and side effects. You want to see it? I left it in here." He opened his black address book.

"Tea doesn't come with prescribing information," she said. She sounded annoyed, like a child. "Prescribing information is for medication."

"It does, this tea does. Do you want to see?" Between two faded Polaroids, in the back cover, he found the yellow piece of paper folded in four.

"Lui? You really don't want to come over? You know..." She laughed again, and this time he imagined her with her mouth open wide, slowly running the tip of her tongue over her lips, chapped from all the smoking. "I think I was a bit shaken by that story with all the deserts, the holes. Lui, do you think the world is ending?"

He unfolded the yellow piece of paper on the table, next to the two pictures. The dark wood of the table had some lighter spots. One of the pictures showed a woman who was almost beautiful, with her hair up and gold earrings shaped like tiny roses. The other was the face of a man wearing a black V-neck, his face resting on one hand, his dark eyes slightly misaligned.

"Not to mention the nuclear power plants," he said. And with the tip of his fingers, he dragged the little pile of ashes on the purple corner over the twisted shapes, brown, yellow, green, to the white part, and, finally, to the face of the man in the picture.

"Lui?" she called out. "Did you find the tea thing?"

"I found it."

"You're acting strange. What is it?"

"Nothing. I'm tired, that's all. Do you want to hear what the leaflet says? It's in English, you'll understand some of it, right?" She didn't answer. He went ahead and read it dramatically. "*...is excellent for all types of nervous disorders, paranoia, schizophrenia, drug effects, digestive problems, hormonal diseases, and other disorders...*"

He laughed, softly, enjoying himself. "Did you understand it?"

"I did," she said. "It's an easy kind of English, anyone can understand it. Impressive, this tea, isn't it? Is it English?"

He continued laughing.

"Chinese. On the bottom here, it says '*Made in China*.'" With the ashes, he covered the man's misaligned eye. "'*Drug effects*' is great, isn't it?"

"Amazing," she said. "That record is playing again. I've already heard this part."

"It's because it all sounds the same like that. Like rain."

"I think I'll turn on the radio."

"Good. Look for a dreamy song." Now he spread the ashes over the nose, where the eyebrows met, thick. "Then you'll doze off, and off, then you're asleep. Almost unconsciously." And unconsciously, he repeated, "Unconsciously."

"All right," she said.

"All right," he repeated. And he thought that when they began talking like this it was already time to hang up, though he didn't want to be the first to do it.

"I'll get it out tomorrow," she said suddenly.

"What?"

"Nothing. Go make your tea."

"OK. It also says here it has vitamin E." He opened his hand and looked at the white spots on his palm. "Isn't that the one that's good for your skin?"

"I think that's A. I don't know much about vitamins."

"C, I know it's for the flu, that everyone knows. Which one do you think cures '*drug effects*'? I've been snorting all day. I have that…high emptiness, you know what that's like?"

"I don't," suddenly she sounded rushed. "I'm hanging up."

"Have you turned on the radio?"

"Not yet. What's the name of that piece again?"

"'For a Pleasant Despair,'" he lied again, then corrected himself. "No. It's just 'Pleasant Despair.'"

"*Pleasant?*"

"Yes. Pleasant. Why not?"

"It's funny. Despair is never pleasant."

"Sometimes it is. Cocaine, for example."

"Is that all you think about?"

"No, I think about making myself some tea as well."

"Huh?"

"But the one that's playing now is different, listen." He held the receiver in the air for a moment, facing the speakers. "They're all very similar. Just the piano, nothing else." The ashes on the photo covered the young man's entire face. "This one is called 'À *L'Occasion d'une Grande Peine*.'"

"Right."

"It's French."

"Right."

"*Peine*-sorrow. Not *peine*-pain. A great sorrow. '*Occasion*' must just mean 'occasion.' But it could be 'passing through.' Better, isn't it? Passing through feels like it's already leaving you, that it's almost over. What do you think?"

"I'll see if I can sleep now," she yawned. "French, English, Chinese tea… You're very cosmopolitan today."

"Escapism," he said. And lit another cigarette.

"It's a shame you don't want to go out. I'm thinking I might open that bottle of vodka anyway."

"Before bed?" he asked. "Have some warm milk. It helps you sleep. Add some cinnamon. And honey. Sugar is bad for you."

"Bad? Look who's talking."

"Do as I say, not as I…"

The ashes were going down his neck, getting mixed up in the black of his shirt. Her voice sounded a bit ironic, almost fierce.

"Oh, now you decide you want to take care of me?"

"I'll go make my tea," he said.

"What was it again? *Esquizofrenia?*"

"It's *schizophrenia*. The stress goes on the *e*, at the end. There's a *cê*, *aitch*. Then there's also a *pê*, another *aitch*. There are two *aitches*."

"And no *uais*? No *dáblius*?" she asked. As if exhausted. And bitter. "I love the *uais*, *dáblius*, and *kahs*. So chic."

"*D'accord*," he said. "But there aren't any."

"OK," she laughed, listlessly. Then said bye, see you, good night, kisses, and hung up.

He opened his mouth, but before he said anything he heard the click of the phone on the hook on the other side of town. The record was ending again, but before it started over, he leaned forward and turned off the stereo. Standing there by the table, he crumpled the yellow piece of paper and threw it in the ashtray. Then he blew the ashes from the man's face. A few specks fell on the picture of the woman. He then walked into the narrow hallway, bent over the plant, and with the ember of his cigarette he made a hole in the leaf. He took a deep breath, no smell in the chill air. The room was still under that burgundy shade, dull, stagnant, with the old yellow cushion shining in the dark, strangely greenish now, in the blue streetlight. He gestured toward the telephone. He even took one step forward, as if he were about to go back. But he didn't move. Standing still in the middle of the house like this, no music playing, he could hear the wind running loose over the tiles of the roof.

Beyond the Point

For Lívio Amaral

It was raining, raining, raining, and I was going into the rain to meet him, no umbrella or anything, I was always losing them in bars. I was holding just a bottle of cheap cognac tight against my chest, hard to believe it said this way, but that was how I was going through the rain, a bottle of cognac in hand and a wet pack of cigarettes in my pocket. At one point I could have taken a cab, but it wasn't very far away, and if I took a cab I couldn't buy cigarettes or cognac. I thought hard, it would be better to get wet, because then we could drink the cognac, it was cold, not that cold, it was more the dampness seeping through the fabric of my clothes, through the holes in the thin soles of my shoes, and we would smoke, would drink without limit, there would be music, always those hoarse voices, that moaning sax, his eye having settled on me, the warm shower loosening my muscles. But it was still raining, my eyes burned from the cold, my nose started dripping, I would wipe it with the back of my hand and the snot would harden quickly over

[43]

my nose hairs, I shoved my reddened hands deep into my pockets and I was going, I was going, jumping over puddles with frigid legs. So frigid my legs and my arms and my face that I thought of opening the bottle to have a sip, but I didn't want to get to his house half drunk, breath stinking, I didn't want him to think that I'd been drinking, and I had been, every day a good excuse, and I was also thinking that he would think I was broke, arriving on foot in all that rain, and I was, stomach aching with hunger, and I didn't want him to think I hadn't been sleeping, and I hadn't, dark circles under my eyes, I would have to be careful with my lower lip when smiling, if I smiled, and I almost certainly would, when I saw him, so that he wouldn't see the broken tooth and think I'd been letting myself go, and I had been, avoiding the dentist, and everything I'd done and been I didn't want him to see or know, but thinking that gave me a heartache because I was realizing, in the rain, that maybe I didn't want him to know that I was me, and I was. A confusing thing started to happen in my head, this idea of not wanting him to know I was me, soaked in that rain that kept falling, falling, falling, I wanted to go back to someplace warm and dry, if there was such a place, and I couldn't remember any, or stay right there forever on that gray intersection I was trying to cross but didn't, the cars splashing rainwater and mud on me as they passed, but I couldn't, or I could have but shouldn't have, or I could have but didn't want to or didn't know how to stop or turn back, I had to keep going to meet him, he would open the door for me, the moaning sax in the background and maybe a fireplace, pine nuts, mulled wine with cinnamon and cloves, those winter things, and even more, I had to stop the urge to turn back or stand still, because there's a point, I was realizing, when you lose control of your own legs, not exactly, the slow realization that the cold and the rain wouldn't even let me chew properly, I was just beginning to learn that there's a point, and I was torn, wanting to see beyond that point and also the pleasure of him waiting for me, hot and ready. A car came closer and drenched me completely, a river would run out of my clothes if I wrung them, so I decided in my head that after opening the door he would say something like, Look how wet you are, with no astonishment, because he was expecting me, he was calling me, I was only going because he was calling me, I dared, I was going beyond the point of staying still, now through the path of leafless trees and that dead-end street I was seeing again in that strange way of having already been there without having been, I hesitated but I was going, through the middle of the city, like an invisible thread coming out of his head up to mine, whoever saw me wet like this couldn't see our secret, only saw a wet guy without a raincoat or umbrella, just a bottle of cheap cognac tight against his chest. It was me he was calling, through the city, pulling the thread from my head to his, in the rain, it was for me that he would open his door, getting very close now, so close I felt a warmth rise up to my face, as if I'd drunk all the cognac, he would change my wet clothes for drier ones and would softly take my hands in his, caressing them slowly to warm them, chasing away the purple of my cold skin, it was getting dark, it was still early, but it was getting dark early, earlier than usual, and it wasn't even winter, he would make a large bed with lots of blankets, and it was then that I slipped and fell, all of a sudden, and to protect the bottle I squeezed it against my chest and it hit a rock, and besides rainwater and mud from the cars now my clothes were also soaked in cognac, like a drunk, stinking, we wouldn't drink it then, I tried to smile, gently, my lower lip almost motionless, hiding the stump of my tooth, and I thought of the mud he would wipe off tenderly, because it was me he was calling, because it was me he was choosing, because it was for me and only for me he would open his door. It kept raining, and it took me a long time to get up from that puddle of mud, I was getting to a point, I was returning to the point, in which an effort so great was necessary, an effort so great was needed, an effort so awful was required that I had to smile even more to myself and invent something more, warming up my secret, and I took a few steps, but how does one do it, I wondered, how does one do this thing of placing one foot in front of the other, balancing the head over the shoulders, keeping the spine erect, I was unlearning, it was nearly nothing, me being held only by that invisible thread attached to my head, now so close that if I wanted to I could imagine something like an electronic buzz coming out of his head until it reached mine, but how does one do it, I was always relearning and inventing, always toward him, to arrive whole, the pieces of me all mixed up, he would lay them out unhurriedly, as if playing with a puzzle to form what castle, what forest, what worm, or god, I didn't know, but I was going in the rain because that was my only reason, my only destination – pounding on that dark door I was pounding on now. And I pounded, and I pounded on it again, and pounded once more, and I kept pounding on it, not caring that people in the street stopped to look, I wanted to call him, but I'd forgotten his name, that is if he'd ever had one at all, maybe I had a fever, everything was very confusing, ideas mixed up, shivering, rainwater and mud and cognac pounding and it still hadn't stopped raining, but I wasn't going in the rain anymore, through the city, I was just standing by that door for a long time, beyond the point, so dark now that I would never be able to find my way back, or try another idea, another action, another gesture beyond pounding pounding pounding pounding pounding pounding pounding pounding pounding pounding pounding pounding pounding on the same door that never opens.

Companheiros
(A Blurry Story)

For Eduardo San Martin

So it could also begin like this: he cleared his throat & said – let's just say he showed or revealed or expressed himself (gave himself over, perhaps?) or what have you, in that particular moment, through his preference, tendency, symbol, symptom, or whatever you want to call it, gentlemen, ladies, to bitter coffee, to strong tobacco, to slow blues, despite this last one being redundant. And the bats fluttered around the house. That's the beginning.

The bats fluttered around the house and the Guy in the Plaid Shirt, who'd been loved and then had stabbed the one who loved him with a knife, tied his hair in a low ponytail. The Guy in the Plaid Shirt still had enough hair on his head to tie up. So it was like that: the Guy in the Plaid Shirt tying up his hair while the bats fluttered around the house, as if in an orgy, a vice, an obsession, as if in an indescribable sadomasochistic ritual. He gave himself over to the bitter blues, the strong coffee, the slow tobacco. Only he hadn't figured out the woman yet because she was so provincial & dark, so he thought he'd go straight into his tran-scen-den-tal talk, and she was on board. Pisces, I could tell right away, ruled by Neptune, ah Neptune, beware of lies, young lady, deep and deceptive like your element the sea. And so years went by.

It's unkind to mention the graffiti, like kill the mother that's inside you, man, my mother is already dying, really, on the real-objective plane, fortunately or unfortunately she exists outside of me (and this is a fact that will never change, and I'll say it again, fact – because everything is fact, it's the only thing that exists, but that's another story), as I was saying, don't evade the fact that there's a story in suspension here, though not really, because stories are never fully suspended: they're consummated in their interruptions, they're full of internal stops, what we imagine to be a continuation sometimes is nothing but a new chapter, sometimes with the same characters as the previous one, but following an order and rules that are on occasion deceptively familiar? or entirely random? I don't know for sure, the truth is that we always end up going too far when we avoid Going Straight to the Facts, and the problem with Going Straight to the Facts is that there's no re-dun-dan-cy then, and most of the time the fun is precisely in these Vain Virtuous Rides, let me put it this way: not that there isn't beauty in the facts as long as we go straight into them? or that there's no mystery, or that it's unbearably unnecessary to like these redundancies? Get past them, I dare you. It just so happens that... No, nothing happens – but please, let's not get into this right now.

The unkindness came from the silence, which was tense and thorny, if polite, so it hurt – though don't expect me to say who it hurt – making things easier with blindness, speed, dizziness: was cruelty the word spoken, and verbs the source of evil? and silence as well and – backtracking a bit – if verbs were evil, the beginning would be Evil and not Good as we'd like to think? Oh. Only on the dirt road up the hill, between the river and the sea, did they finally start enjoying themselves a little, thinking themselves laid back. The Shaman had dark curly hair that brought out her dramatic features, along with a Certain Wounded Air of Someone Past Her Thirties Who'd Been Through a Lot. And she was actually quite nice, the Fortune-Telling Journalist prosaically observed between two swigs of wine, two puffs of the old familiar bitter cigarette. The Buffoon Actor played his role in the background with paradoxical efficiency, often a little too loud, but harmless as buffoons often are, even when they try to get smart.

That was how things were going when – and there was almost nothing else to add, because nothing ever happened between them, except for, using a certain sense of nor-ma-tiv-ity and not necessarily in this order: a) Indefinable Climates; b) Indescribable Subtleties; c) Horrible Affectation. Or so they were called.

Horrible with a capital H, because even without having to justify this entirely: affectation in excess gnaws at you from the inside, that was a consequence of the lesson that was established in that bedroom. As if underneath the long arm of an immaculate white glove, behind the lace and the stitches, were twisted claws, slender like gothic towers, scratching the glass of a closed window in the dark.

But so it was. He walked down the streets without touching the streets, he could do that. He moved between mirrors.

Walking down the street: infinity game. The now taking him back to the before, which reflected the after, a bit too similar to the now, and so forth, in circular fashion, *ad infinitum*. Everything reflecting itself. Each reflection returned something that wasn't that street exactly. That one, where he walked. One could argue against Him that this was just another way of not committing.

One of those Horrible Affectations, because accepting or acknowledging a lesson didn't necessarily mean a change in how you act. But it meant that in that moment, in that suspended fact where nothing happened, suddenly and for no reason, the Shaman (once a guerrilla fighter), the Buffoon Actor (a seminar dropout), and the Fortune-Telling Journalist (with roots in the counterculture) weren't concerned or embarrassed about being Caricaturally Representative of a Generation, whichever one it was. The truth was loud and clear, though only in writing: they were intensely happy when nothing happened. At least until they heard the bats outside again. Of course they weren't aware of that – of their happiness, not of the ominous bats – and maybe they would never be; exactly for this reason it needed to be said, no one would understand it but at least there's a record of it, for the benefit of nothing and no one. Fully being what they were, they breathed, sufffused with innocent humanity.

And all this was happening without happening exactly, while the Provincial & Dark Woman, if you looked close enough, which was hard to do, kept some depth behind her provincialism, and if you looked even closer, she didn't even look that dark. It was exhausting, even without any words between them, at least not there, which was the only place where you might reach them. It was unfathomable too, to someone who'd never been part of something like that. But comforting, even if they weren't drinking tea. As comforting as re-unions tend to be, anyway. Or as they should usually be, since most of the time they're all discomfort, even with tea.

Except for the bats, fuck, they kept circling them, even though it was summer and the house had once been white and the patch of grass outside had held delightful recuerdos of sunny afternoons with colorful bouncy balls and baby dogs jumping up and down at the feet of quite old women, naturally in bloom, with their lacy outfits and ankle socks spilling over their little patent leather shoes, hula hoops & yo-yos abandoned on the worn front steps. It had a taste of all of this, the house. But he didn't believe it enough to justify the bats' presence, or was it only a suspicion? because even, unforgivable flaw in this story, if the house had a dusty attic, sinis-ter basements, banana trees in the backyard. After thinking about it some more, he still didn't know, it had been too many years, if reality was really magic or just paranoia, depending on the disposition of each one to dig into their wound.

He preferred, then, to look at her in the mirror, like when he walked down the street. This took him back to older wounds, neither more nor less painful, because the memory of the pain of the oldwound has since faded, you know? An oldwound is more accurately measured by the pain caused than by the scar left behind, and it's forever lost in the moment it stopped hurting, though it still throbs angrily on rainy days. Which is probably healthy. The Provincial & Dark Woman would never presume him immersed in such useless cerebral exercises, and there wasn't a drop of complicity between the Guy in the Plaid Shirt and the Fortune-Telling Journalist anymore, since that would imply some kind of sublimated homoeroticism, if I am making myself clear in the middle of this mess. Like moral intercourse, or an ethical or ethereal fuck, who knows to what exquisite levels of abstraction, perversity, or evasion certain fucks can get to. He considered his wounds, while totally submerged in the slow blues, strong tobacco, and bitter coffee, which was sometimes replaced by cognac (dense) or wine (dry). Between one word or another, he was capable of stopping himself so he could take some objective measures, like emptying the ashtrays changing the records serving the drinks opening the windows then shutting them right after, quickly, to keep out the bats.

As for the Shaman, she also showed cigarette scars on her

tortured skin, especially on her breasts and thighs, in a kind of reverse seduction, through ideology, not aesthetics, but only when in the most absolute intimacy, when all possibility of fitting into any kind of Leninist-Trotskyist exhibitionism had been discarded. Although, like wrinkles and losses, scars were also trophies. Big failures, like Napoleon's Waterloo, deserve to be rewarded, after all, why all this Manichaean discrimination? demanded the Buffoon Actor, from time to time taking the reins and hurling words – he was a very good buffoon, it must be said – like several balls up in the air. He was capable of (dis)ordering them in infinite combinations, such as two red ones over his head, a purple one in his left hand, a blue one in his right hand, and that yellow one going under his right leg, or the left, it doesn't matter, and that moss-green, also up in the air at the same time. The Buffoon Actor's biggest problem was that all his talents weren't worth a cent, given that nowadays not a lot of people are interested in bizarre combinations of colorful jug-gl-ing balls.

He lowered his eyes. Wounds, scars, desires – he chewed, they chewed. Against the closed window (to keep out the bats), the Provincial & Dark Woman next to the Shaman looked like a slightly matured Capitu asking Catherine of Wuthering Heights for advice. The only one who wasn't one bit aware of his own presence, or any parameters, was the Guy in the Plaid Shirt, who'd been so loved and then had stabbed the one who loved him with a knife: he remained very still, suspended between several things that weren't anymore and some others that might come to be, or not. While nothing happened, he tied his hair in a low ponytail, given that he still had some hair, though this was another decade, with other delusions. He tied his hair this way, and now it was so clear, because perhaps this was his silent victory, his implicit advantage, in a moment when, in addition to no further growth, everyone else had either cut off or lost all their hair. They'd gotten to a point where speaking about the bats could ruin everything, even though there was nothing to be ruined. Even though there weren't any bats.

It should also be said that, despite the hollow sound of wings, the tiny shrieks cutting the air, the sticky claws – no gloves or lace – scratching the glass of a closed window, even from time to time looking straight into their eyes drenched in alcohol and drugs for years, they wouldn't dare speak of the bats. Or it's not that they wouldn't dare: the bats might have been unspeakable, for in not being spoken about, and shared, each one of them suspected they were personal & untransferable, you know? What I mean is that by not speaking about the bats, the bats didn't exist, and then became what they weren't: metaphors of themselves.

As such (it's all so logical), no obscure tensions hovered over the Guy in the Plaid Shirt, the Provincial & Dark Woman, the Buffoon Actor, the Shaman, and the Fortune-Telling Journalist, all without any real reason to be there in that moment like that, seated on the

Frustrated Marine's bedroom rug, who'd been away, though he still left the polished anchors and the gleaming models of transatlantic ships in their places, some of them inside bottles. Also away was the Ideal Husband, since his function in life was actually to strategically disappear without leaving a trace, which had its dose of nostalgia, but also of relief, it must be said. Like the bookcase of dark wood holding the weight of the complete works Karl May, Michel Zevaco, and Edgar Rice Burroughs.

In the middle of summer, a chilly breeze blew unexpectedly up the stairs.

In those moments, when the blues became even slower, the sound of the bats became even more noticeable. In those moments, they contemplated each other's sneakers in a messy pile, even if they were barefoot, and considered undeniable facts like the stack of dirty plates in the kitchen sink. Going Straight to the Facts now would be for example running without a single comma to the sink armed with the most hygienic intentions & a good biodegradable detergent. Or turning the record over to release an even more anguished blues, almost unbearably pained, each note from the sax lasting at least as long as Genesis. Until the Provincial & Dark Woman sank her teeth into an imaginary apple so they'd in a way be banished from paradise. And thus would grow heather and thistles and thorns and they would feed themselves with weeds and would eat bread seasoned with sweat of their brows – because such is the nature of cycles, he'd comment didactically, though a little fatigued and already a bit dull, the Buffoon Actor. The others, perhaps, would say nothing. Or would make no movement, an even more silent way of saying nothing.

At the same time, for all of them, it was extremely convenient and perfectly unbearable staying like this, in the middle of their stillness, milling bats fluttering behind the closed windows of that bedroom where perhaps the anchored anchors on the wall might offer something like – a direction? And finally, for a long series of vague deep dull silly or even more confused reasons, this kind of thing was basically all that could be said about them. Slow like this, bitter, dead, strong, even. Surviving death from all the omens.

Fat Tuesday

For Luiz Carlos Góes

Suddenly, he started to dance beautifully and walk toward me. He looked me in the eye with a discreet smile, a tense wrinkle between his brows, asking for reciprocity. I gave it to him, with a discreet smile as well, my mouth sticky from all the warm beer, vodka with coke, cheap whiskey, tastes I couldn't even discern anymore, going from hand to hand in plastic cups. He was wearing a red and white loincloth, Shango, I thought, Oya with glitter on his face, Obatala holding his sword in his arms, Ogun dancing so beautifully and provocatively. A quick movement that fell like a wave from his hips, through his thighs, to his feet, before he looked down and the movement rose again, through his waist, all the way to his shoulders. Then he shook his head, looking at me, coming even closer.

I was all sweaty. Everyone was sweaty, but I saw no one apart from him. I'd seen him before, though not there. A while ago, I can't remember where. I'd been to so many places. He'd probably been to many places too. At one of those places, perhaps. Here and there. Though we didn't realize this until we finally spoke, maybe not even then. We had no words. There was only movement, sweat, his body and mine coming close, not wanting anything besides getting closer to each other's warmth.

As he stood in front of me, we stared at each other. Now I was dancing too, following his movement: hips, thighs, feet, looking down for a moment, the wave rising through my waist all the way to my shoulders, then shaking my wet hair, raising my head, and looking at him with a smile. His sweaty chest met mine. We had hairy chests, both of us. Our wet hair mixed together. He stretched out his open hand, touched my face, said something or other. What? I asked. You're hot, he said. He didn't even look queer or anything: just a body that happened to be masculine enjoying another body, mine, that happened to be masculine too. I stretched out my open hand, touched his face, said something or other. What? he asked. You're hot, I said. I was just a body that happened to be masculine enjoying another body, his, that happened to be masculine too.

I wanted that man's body dancing sweaty and beautiful in front of me. I want you, he said. I said, I want you too. But I want you right now at this very moment, he said, and I said it too, I want that too. He smiled wider, showing his bright teeth. He stroked my stomach. I stroked his. He grabbed, we grabbed. Our flesh covered with hair and firm with muscles under the tan skin. Ai ai, someone said in falsetto, look at them queens, and walked away. Around us, people stared.

His mouth came closer to mine, slightly open. Like a ripe fig cut into quarters, the pulp slowly torn from the round side to the tip with the blade of a knife, revealing the pink insides full of seeds. Did you know, I asked, that figs aren't fruit, that they're actually flowers that bloom inward? What? he yelled. Figs, I repeated. But it didn't matter. He reached into his swimming trunks and took out two little pills in a silver sleeve. He took one and offered me the other. No, I said, I wanted my lucidity no matter what. But I was completely crazy. And I desired that little ball of chemicals, warm from his crotch. I stuck out my tongue, swallowed it. Someone in the crowd pushed us, I tried to shield him with my body, but ai ai, they repeated, still pushing us, look at them queens. Let's go, he said. We left glued to one another across the dance floor, the glitter on his face sparkling in between shouts.

Fags, we heard as we welcomed the cold sea breeze. The music was just a thump-thump-thump of feet and drums beating. I looked up and pointed, look at the Pleiades, the only constellation I knew how to identify, like a tennis racket hanging from the sky. You'll catch a cold, he said, his hand on my shoulder. That was when I noticed we weren't wearing masks. I remembered reading somewhere that pain is the only emotion that doesn't wear a mask. We weren't in pain, but the emotion we felt at that moment, and I don't even know if it was joy, didn't wear a mask either. I thought then that it must be forbidden or dangerous not to wear masks, especially during Carnival.

His hand squeezed my shoulder. My hand squeezed his waist. Sitting on the sand, he took out a piece of paper, a round mirror, a razor blade from his magic trunks. He cut four lines, snorted two, offered me the rolled-up bill. I snorted deep, one in each nostril. I licked the glass, I wet my gums. Throw the mirror to Yemanjá, he said. The mirror glinted in the air, and while I followed its flight I grew afraid of looking at him again. Because if you blink, when you open your eyes again the pretty might turn ugly. Or vice versa. Look at me, he asked. And I did.

We were glowing, both of us, looking over at one another on the sand. I feel like I know you from somewhere, man, he said, or maybe it's just me. It doesn't matter, I said. He said, don't say anything, then hugged me tight. I looked at his face up close, which seen from this angle was neither beautiful nor ugly: pores and hair, a real face looking up close at another real face that happened to be mine. His tongue went down my neck, my tongue into his ear, before they melded together, wet. Like two ripe figs pressed tight against one another, the red seeds grating against one another like teeth against teeth.

We took off each other's clothes, then rolled in the sand. I won't ask your name, your age, your number, your sign, your address, he said. His hard nipple in my mouth, my hard dick in his hand. If you tell me a lie I'll believe you, I said, as if quoting an old Carnival song. We kept rolling in the sand up to where the waves crashed, so the water would wash the sweat and sand and glitter off our bodies. We held each other tight. We wanted to hold each other tight like this because we completed each other this way, one body as the other body's missing half. So simple. Classic, even. We pulled away a little, just to look at how beautiful our naked masculine bodies looked stretched on the sand beside each other, gleaming with phosphorescence from the waves. Planktons, he said, they glow when they make love.

And we glowed.

Then they came, and they were many. Run, I shouted, stretching out my arm. My hand grabbed nothing. The kick in my back got me up. He stayed on the ground. They were all around us. Ai ai, they yelled, look at them queens. Looking down, I saw his eyes wide-open and guiltless, among all the other faces. His wet mouth drowning in that dense mass, a loose tooth glinting on the sand. I wanted to take him by the hand, shield him with my body, but suddenly, without planning to, I was running alone on the wet sand, the others all around us, too close.

As I shut my eyes I saw three images juxtaposed, like a movie under my lids. First his sweaty body, dancing, walking in my direction. Then the Pleiades like a tennis racket up there in the sky. And finally, the slow fall of an overripe fig, until it met the ground in a thousand bloody pieces.

I, You, He

For Raquel Salgado

I touch, you touch, he touches. Or: we touch, you and I, we grope our way in the dark as he swans around the room? I know very little about you, I merely suspect you exist, since the moment I realized that neither he nor I are the owners of certain words. Like I finally noticed a blank space between he and I, and then – out of alienation, intuition, invention – sensed you, the owner of this space between his light and my dark. Do you touch, too? About you, I barely know anything. But you balance out the pure shadow that is between him and me.

I am going away, I am leaving, and I need you to understand before I go, crucified on the back of a train at high speed. I try again, slower and louder: but he doesn't go away. Day after day, I notice, he becomes nicer, more efficient, more solicitous – always smiling a lot, always bowing to others, head always down, like a geisha. Geisha, him, that grand old slut, with her silence of tiny steps and bound feet. I need to try to establish a certain order to what I'm saying here, and say it again, see if you can understand me: he's not going away, but it's inside him that I'm going away. From inside him, I take a peek outside. And I do not dare.

What I see in others, with their big open pores, are faces full of vigor. Those faces on the outside lean forward and I am afraid, I could never look straight into all those irises floating on viscous whiteness, webbed with red veins, and I feel disgusted. Not by the eyes, but by the insides of those faces, showing through the veins. Also not by the mouths, but by the gummy redness inside when they're wide open. The countless black dots on the noses, sometimes going all the way up to the forehead, between the eyebrows, the pink inside the noses, the open throats with their moving wetness, full of little spasms, tiny convulsions. When the vigorous faces lean forward, I feel that I also show through the thin veins, and I fear that a blink of an eye could push me out, among sharp edges. And when he opens his quicksand mouth to spit words out, drops of saliva and bad breath, I fear him being just this word, this drop, this breath. Just as when he rubs his palms against one another and releases his beams of energy in the air, as if he were a vibration, not a being.

I can always stop, look beyond the window. But from inside the train, the view is never still. The colorful ipe trees blend with the concrete walls, and the concrete walls with the narrow streets of discolored houses, and the streets of discolored houses with the faces of women washing clothes by the river, and all the way from the train their faces are neither moving nor vigorous, but featureless, carved in clay over bundles of dirty clothes, and once more the purple and yellow of the ipe trees and the brown of the earth, and the burgundy of the bougainvillea and the green of the military uniform crossing the tracks. There's an excess of colors and shapes in the world. And everything vibrates and pulses, trembling.

From that last afternoon of light, what I still remember is the sticky cold sweat on my palms, the countless glimmering dots from the passing cars, my expression shattered with the noise. The cars were colorful, metallic sparks hovering over the asphalt. I pressed my dizziness with my wet palms, not sure if I should go, or turn back, or quietly stay still in the middle of the crazy flashes of light spinning around me. I must have started to scream, because he suddenly sealed his mouth shut, not letting me escape through his closed throat.

But was it you, or him, or me, that the man sometimes visited? Whose tongue was it that explored the deepest of all the orifices of his body with no disgust? From my window, I watched the hands hurriedly unzipping the pants, the skilled fingers parting the fabric, the nostrils breathing in the secret scent of his groin. The man's big and vigorous body. From behind the bars, I wanted those hands, mine, that touched him and also those fingers, mine, and even those nostrils, mine, and that tongue licking his hard member, until it was erect enough to very carefully enter ripping him with pleasure and pain. Was it you, me, or him, who slowly twisted the body until collapsing in bed, clasping the man's waist and butt with our thighs and feeling him inside me, you, him, the way a woman feels her man, face to face, never the way a man receives another man, face against the nape of the neck, in this love made of sperm and hair, of sweat and shit? Behind his window, I looked without fully allowing myself. But our orgasm was the same, and in that moment we were one, us three, ridden by this man we exhausted with the thirst of our tongues. In moments like this, I knew your face as intimately as I knew his and my own. And the big open pores didn't scare me anymore, and all that slime from the orifices didn't disgust me.

As for you, have you noticed how the world is all corners and edges? Have I called your attention to the scarcity of gentle shapes in the world? Everything is hard, and wounds. I notice, you notice how he moves without incident between the edges. Does he seem sweet to you, coiled like this, avoiding any touch that could hurt him? Because to me it looks forced. I'm very familiar with his plots and I know of each time he gave in so the outside wouldn't hurt him. Look, listen, and observe: these are the coils of a snake, not those of a bird.

Only sometimes do I feel that I understand. Then I want to open every window in the house to let the sun come in. That's what I think of doing every morning, always at the same time, as I hear the sounds he makes before heading out the door. I listen attentively to the water running through the tap, the brush grating against his teeth, the water in the toilet taking to the sewer the crap rejected by his intestines, the water washing the signs of sleep from the corners of his eyes, the cold water from the shower invigorating his muscles, the hot water for his coffee, I listen to it all. And water, water, water, and water, I repeat to myself each morning, and even if I spend the rest of the day under the sheets, my hand inventing hidden pleasures between my legs, there's always a part of me that goes with him on the busy streets, on the dirty path catching the metallic sparks from the cars, as he doles out his first fake smiles of the day, out and about, following his well-plotted script without any hesitation. He knows what he wants, that pig. And knows exactly how to get it. Out, and about, this part of me that goes with him tries to escape through his eyes, through his mouth, to warn the friendly moving faces that observe him. Each time he senses my presence and rejects it, pushes me deeper into himself so I won't unmask him. And he steals my voice, takes away my gestures, so I am silenced and paralyzed, powerless between the hard corners he dodges, that dancing pig, capable of the dirtiest tricks for the big solo. I go unwitnessed as I unmask him each morning, while I hear the water running, meant to wash away all the dirt. But I watch you, I search you, I suspect you're my accomplice, not his, because your help is the only thing I can expect, so I always insist and ask, do you understand me? so, you understand, me? do you, now, or ever?

It was always pleasant when that woman came with her charts, her graphs, her drafting compasses to talk about the movement of the stars above our heads, wise and distracted, drawing pyramids, triangles, spheres, and diamonds on the grid paper. It was on one of these early visits that he tried to send her away, laughing rudely, the way people laugh at stuff like this, always choosing pigs over birds. Was it you who helped me violently shut his mouth until his teeth ground to the point of breaking that one time? Because that effort wasn't only mine, I found out, and perhaps that was the first time I noticed your presence parallel to mine, and to his. But perhaps chronologies don't matter, if we coexisted even before my knowledge of you. As for the woman, she kept on coming, always said that when the Moon is in Aquarius... But I never knew about constellations: all I did was welcome her, and she seemed like a girl full of faith in everything that she suspected was real, even if invisible.

All my days are like an anticipation of my departure. I move between corners as someone who knows that soon he won't be present anymore. The suitcase has been packed, the farewells have been bid. Walking from one end to the other of the train platform, all there is for me to do is look at things, sluggish and sad, emotionless, no desire to stay. The shutters open, the benches look like benches, and vases hold flowers in their depths. Things look the way they are. Nothing will change the presence of things in the world, and my departure yesterday, today, or tomorrow, won't change a thing. Each thing looks exactly the way each thing is. And so I too look like myself, walking back and forth, between flavorless cigarettes, bleeding newspapers, and the certainty that the only thing that would prevent my departure is your accepting this invitation: don't you want to help me kill him?

One day, the man didn't come anymore. And not knowing if it had been me, you, or him that sent him away, that day I wrote something like a prayer that sounded ridiculous to me. But revisiting these notes now, it pulses as if the words had been stabbed, and I realize now, it sounds as if it had also been written for you, for him, and for me. This:

I'm not waiting for this man who is not only this one but all men and none like a thirst for something I've never drunk something that doesn't have the shape of water only the narrowness of the here and now and I've been waiting for him since the day I was born and since then I've known that at the time of my death mixing up memories and hallucinations and premonitions a little while ago the last thing I would ask you would be a but where are you but where have you been this entire time I was hurting without you and to cheer me up afterward maybe you'd give up or give me a beautiful smile with no teeth a bright smile in the darkness of my mouth a broad smile that had never been possible before and spit out anything, something like, so you've always been living a searching life without ever finding yourself and silence so I can die now a dead death no

coming back to this life spent marked with so many scars
carved by so many wounds but none of them lethal to the
point of stopping this ridiculousness till the hour of my death
amen.

But this face of mine, newly awakened, slowly refreshed and without a single sigh, because there's nothing to mourn, it crudely thinks, this barefaced face: so let's not part ways, the three of us. When I believe I'm out, I'm in. And when I guess I'm in, I'm out. Of you or him, of me in me, embedded triplicity, though it might seem confusing I think about it this way, and it is nearly clear as the city roars in the background and I lean this body of ours over the seven overpasses: embedded triplicity, strange triplicity, intertwined triplicity. Triplicity forever conjoined, the death of one the death of all three, I don't want you to help me kill him because it would kill you and also me. I recompose myself, I recompose you, and I recompose him, who is also me and also you.

The woman said that the Moon was in Scorpio, and told me: no teeth, torn, bits of puke hardened and stuck to his chest hair, the man followed her. Before I could touch her, she found the little white animal with its pink snout, and grabbing a piece of wood she beat it, she beat it and beat it until the creature was a mash of blood and broken bones and hair, where a pair of open eyes that wouldn't die also floated. I told her: through the tree trunk, from one end of the cliff to the other, I crossed it. That was when I stopped, afraid of the abyss. I wouldn't turn back, or go forward. Then I looked at the face of that cliff and saw a bunch of grapes hanging from a vine and my fear started to dissipate because I wouldn't go hungry and I wouldn't die, because the harvest would come soon, a ripe time for grapes. Oneirically, we exchanged dreams between the two of us, the three of us, the four. And the woman trapped in the woman's body called for me, for you, for him, not minding that we were three. She knew and wanted the three of us. Before she left, she wrote on the graph paper, looking at each of us, keep this: the other one also searches blindly, the other one too, and they're always three.

A while later – now, I realize: it's through the dark hallways of a maze that we grope our way, the three of us, searching for the vertex. I know you don't understand, and I know he also doesn't. About your day, I barely know anything, but I know about the maze in you, as I know about his maze in me, of my maze in you. I don't understand you either.

I need to stop. I'm tired. This light that could be either enlightenment or madness fills my head. Is it from me, from you, or from him that comes this voice retelling yesterday's dream? As if it were all you, you go into the theater and they invite you to play the role of someone else's dream, someone who isn't present, and you say that you've never seen the play and never read the script and that you know nothing about interpreting intentions interiorizations and they tell you that it doesn't matter because it's just a dream and a dream needs no rehearsing, and you don't know if you start to laugh or to scream, so you run away to meet someone, but the woman's face has the man's eyes and the woman's mouth, the woman's breasts are the woman's breasts, the same ones, with the hardened nipples that brushed against your untrimmed beard when you kissed them, but the woman's sex is the man's sex, that same one that flooded you with warm sperm, and you feel neither fear nor disgust, but you move away, confused, and you walk and you walk, searching for the theater to go into the scene and perform your dream of someone else's dream as well as you can, then you search and search inside the theater, in pyramids of narrow hallways, and you continue searching for the stage, the vertex, the royal chamber, your cue, your mark, and before waking up you don't think, or you think, yes, I don't know, he doesn't know, you don't know, and no one else knows either if perhaps you're lost and haven't memorized your lines, because the stage is the search for the stage and your role is not knowing the role and everything's alright and the visible disorder is suddenly ordered and the great order of all things is chaos, spinning disordered the way chaos must, and so I dive and so you dive and so he dives: the dizziness of our six steps as our balance gets more stable and precise over the razor's edge. But – I know, you know, we know – the grapes might take too long to ripen. And we're almost out of time.

Light and Shadow

In memory of Juan Carlos Chacón

There must be some sort of meaning, or what would come after? This is the kind of stuff I'm thinking about this afternoon, standing here by the window, facing the endless zinc roofs where doves sometimes land, cooing. They're gray, the doves, and the sound they make is sinister like the sound of bat wings. I know bats really well, their sharp shrieks, screeches. But let's not get ahead of ourselves. I think that if I manage to make some sense out of what I'm saying, I will also, therefore, make some meaning. At the same time, or maybe right after, I think that I don't know for sure that after this sense and meaning comes anything else.

What will come after? I ask the dirty afternoon behind the glass, and I feel comforted like there's something resembling a future ahead of me. As if I'd just finished my tea and now was slowly smoking a minty cigarette, staring into the distance like this, warm from the tea, calm from the cigarette, enraptured by the distance and above all alert to what would come after this moment. It's been a while since I've had a cup of tea, and I limit the cigarettes I smoke so much that every time I light one, the feeling is all guilt, not pleasure, you know what I mean?

No, you don't know. I know you don't know because I'm not being clear enough, and because I'm not clear enough, besides keeping you in the dark, I'm unable to make any sense of this myself. So there won't be meaning, so there won't be an after. Before making myself understand, if I can at all, I'd like to at least make you understand me, before one word, forget everything, pretend we just started talking, at this moment and with this sentence I'm about to say. This: it's all very trying for me. If I stay here, standing by this window, I'm certain something grave will happen – and when I say *grave*, I mean *death*, *madness*, which sound way too light said like this. I need someone to take me away from this window and then right after, still, away from the after. Wanting a meaning leads me to wanting an after. These two cling together, if you know what I mean.

I was talking about the window. I could start there, then.

It's a large window, made of glass. Floor to ceiling, it doesn't open, air-tight. The room is very small, there's nothing in it but the moss-green carpet, which makes me sick to my stomach. And now something occurs to me: I believe I stared out the window so I wouldn't throw up so much and so often, with my back to the carpet like this.

So, the roofs.

Don't ask me how or why, but the window doesn't face the street like most windows do, but instead faces those endless zinc roofs I mentioned. Yes, yes, I tried to be interested in the stains on the zinc, the small crinkles, the ripples and all that. And really I was interested, at first. But the roofs are endless, you know. No, you don't, you don't know how much I've tried to be interested in something this uninteresting. And so began again that feeling of nausea: the roofs extending across the horizon, like an enormous green carpet. Before I threw up looking at the roofs, fortunately came the doves. But like I said: they're gray, the sound they make is like the sound of bat wings. Their beaks constantly hit the glass. Were there no glass, they'd hit my face. So I won't throw up, I try to look beyond the roofs sinking into infinity. I don't see anything, just the heavy gray sky and the soot slowly gathering on the windowsill. At dusk, the soot gains new pink shades, and shortly after, when darkness descends, comes that moment when I have to curl up on the carpet and finally sleep.

In the morning, every day, someone puts a piece of bread through the crack in the door, a tin can with water, like I'm a dog, and a pack of cigarettes. I don't know who it is. I hear them constantly grinding their teeth, which perhaps might be just another way of smiling. I think they used to smoke a lot, the room is full of ashes at least, of cigarette butts, because there's no ashtray and it's impossible to open the window, are you listening to me?

It doesn't matter. When it's very hot, I often have a vision. I don't know if it's a memory or a vision. Either way, when it's very hot, I see something clearly.

It's three o'clock on a January afternoon. I'm sitting on a cement stoop. There are three steps between the dirt road lined with some weeds, maybe nettle, and the very tall and old doorway, with the brown paint peeling off. I'm sitting on the second step by this door. I know it's three o'clock because the shadows are short and the sun is very bright. I know it's January because it's very hot. There are no clouds in the sky. The street is deserted. The street is covered with a layer of crumbly soil, red. Across the street is a stone wall. Nothing happens.

I can see the tops of the cinnamon trees across the street, but they're still. There's no wind. I know that beyond the stone wall, further down, there's a river. The afternoon is so hot and bright that I'd like to walk to that river. But in order to do that I'd need to get up. There's a soft shade on me, enough to make sure I won't get too warm. I'm barefoot. I don't know how old I am, but I must not be a teenager yet, because my legs still don't have any hair. Because I'm barefoot, perhaps, I don't dare step onto the loose soil, red, in the middle of the street.

There are glass shards too, green glass shards in the middle of the soil on the street, which the sun makes glint until it hurts my eyes. Sometimes I place my hand above my forehead like a visor. I'm good, like this. There's so much light I need to strain my eyelids to be able to look straight ahead. The January heat warms my body.

I cross my arms over my knees. This feels good. I'm almost certain that on the other side of the brown door, someone is running something like a cold bath or the coffee maker. And even though the street is deserted, I don't feel alone here on the stoop, this afternoon.

On the hot nights of such hot days, I usually have another vision. I'm not on the stoop anymore, but behind that same door, inside the house. Maybe years have gone by, maybe it's only the night of that same day. There's no light. The floor is very cold. I think I'm in a bedroom, there are mosquito nets hanging from the ceiling. I'm not sure they're mosquito nets because there's no movement. I think then they could also be spider webs, and I prefer not to reach for them and touch them – the tulle, the mesh – to confirm. I prefer not to confirm anything. Through the blinds comes a thin line of blue light. There are voices outside. I imagine they might be sitting in front of the house, on that hot summer night. From time to time, I imagine, a shooting star. I'm good like this, as good as I was on the stoop.

I don't know how long it lasts, or where it all begins. Little by little my ears distinguish the voices outside from the sharp screeches getting louder around me, and right after that I feel the wings brushing against face. I don't know from where, bats have come into the room. Without meaning to, I think about the ceiling. I can't see it in the dark, but somehow I know it's made of thin pieces of wood, over the brick washed white. The bats flutter around, I don't move. Some hit the walls, then fall onto the floor shrieking sharply, shrill. Then I'm the one who screeches. Motionless, eyes closed, I screech, screech, and screech until it's over, and suddenly I find myself curled up on the green carpet, face against the glass, staring at the endless roofs through the glass.

At this hour, the soot in the sky has those pink shades. Dawn is breaking. By the door, the bread, the tin can with water, the pack of cigarettes. When I pick them up, even if I look ahead or look up, the green from the carpet stifles me and I throw up. I'm not always fast enough to move, twist my hips, and make sure the vomit doesn't fall on the bread, the water, the pack of cigarettes. And when I throw up all over them, I always hear the teeth grinding behind the door. On those days I don't eat, don't drink, don't smoke. Just walk over to the window, and as the pink dissolves into gray again, the doves pecking at my face shielded by glass, I repeat like this – there must be some sort of meaning, or what would come after?

I don't cry anymore. Actually, I don't even understand why I say *anymore*, if I'm not certain I've ever cried. I believe I have, at one point. When there was pain. Now there's only dryness. Inside, out.

Sometimes I close my eyes and have the impression that these endless roofs are the only thing that exist inside me, do you understand me now? What? Yes, I do want to throw myself out the window, but it's impossible to open it. *Sleep*, perhaps, or *it's alright*, or even *don't think about it, don't think about it*. I can't. When I puke on the bread, I can't eat or puke anymore. I like to puke, it feels a little bit like being able to cry. Perhaps you could at least teach me a way to puke without having to eat first? Despite my growing nails, they're not long enough to stick down my throat. Yes, I must have read this in some book. Even though I've said this, it must be the only way. I'd like to avoid it.

Inside me, I can't stop thinking that there must be some sort of meaning. And an after. When I think about it, it's like someone is dancing on the endless roofs from inside me. On the gray roofs someone dressed entirely in yellow. I don't know why yellow exactly, but it shines. The wind would blow the clothes and hair. With a long leap, this someone would reach the window and open it with the soft touch of a finger. I'm almost certain it must be you.

No, don't say anything. I'd rather not know that it's not. Or that it is. Do you despise me for just lying here like this? Again, don't say anything. I can't see your face clearly because the clothes and the hair cover you entirely, blown by the wind. I also know that, after the leap, you would take me by the hand so I'd finally leave that stoop, crossing the street of hot loose red dirt, perhaps, to go together into that river's fresh water. I also know that you'd take me out of that dark room, brush off the veils and webs, so we could sit in front of the house, without the others, looking at the vertical descent of the stars on that hot January night.

I'd like to think that this is meaning, that it'll be the after. I don't know if I can. There are days, like today, when it doesn't matter how much I lie, I still can't see you, the wind blowing your clothes against your long limbs. I only hear the grinding of the teeth and the sounds coming from my own body. All of this blinds me. Take me out of here, I ask. And cross my arms over my chest, like I'm cold or fending off demons. I press my face against the glass. Two doves, each one pecking at one of my eyes. Maybe one day they'll manage to break the glass. Without meaning to, I think of an old fairy tale: two doves prick the eyes of two evil sisters, do you remember it? There are fairies in that story. There's no one dancing on the roofs. There has never been. To evade the gray that turns into green, I look beyond it.

It's very hot today. When the time comes, I know I'll find myself sitting on that stoop again. And after the gray has turned into pink then purple then deep blue then finally black, I know I'll be standing in the middle of that room again, listening to the sharp shrieks and batting of wings. I'll screech, then. Very loud, with all my strength, for a long time. I don't know if this will be the order of the events, or if it'll be like this at all. But I know for sure that neither you nor anyone else will hear me.

Strawberries

Give me some more wine, because life is nothing.
                    —Fernando Pessoa, *Cancioneiro* [*Songbook*]

Those who know God
feel what's inside
and are friends of the strawberries
that never die.

                    —Henrique do Valle, "Os morangos são eternos"
                    ["Strawberries are Forever"]

Transformations
(A Fable)

For Domingos Lalaina Jr.

Like a fever, sometimes he was struck with the feeling that nothing in his life would ever go well, all efforts would always be futile and nothing would ever change. More than a feeling, it was a dense and viscous certainty that blocked any movement toward the light. And beyond that certainty, it was a premonition of a future where there wouldn't be the faintest outline of any hope, faith, joy, anything.

Those days were full of stillness. No matter how much he went through the motions of his day – waking up, eating, walking, sleeping – something inside him remained still. Like his body was just the frame of a drawing of a face, quietly resting over a hand, eyes fixed in the distance. He'd gone somewhere, they'd say when they saw him, if they saw him. And that wouldn't be true at all. He was as present as ever on those days, so full and close, he was inside what he'd call – if he had the words, which he didn't, or didn't wish to find them – vaguely and precisely: The Great Absence.

It was translucent and cold. If it had eyes, they'd certainly be green, with distant pupils. He once found a shard from a glass bottle by the shore, so pristinely chiseled by the waves, sands, and winds, it glinted in the sun, precious cheap jewel. He squeezed it between his fingers and felt the anesthetic cold, which prevented him from noticing the drops of blood blooming, warm in the palm of his hand. The Great Absence was like that. If they could see him, if he could see himself, they'd see the blood, he and the others. It's just that he became invisible on those days. He looked at himself in the mirror, and immediately knew he was inside It. Through the glass, beyond himself, he could only see a pale green reflection.

The Great Absence was as deep inside him as he was inside It. They were intertwined to the point of one turning into the depth and surface of the other. Sometimes this eased off throughout the day, clouds dissipating, cloudy water clearing up as the night fell surprisingly sharp, cleaned up, ironed out. Then he smiled, made phone calls, sang songs, or went to the movies. But other times, it got thicker, as dark as the sky, turbulent cloudiness rising up from the bottom, fogged-up glass. Unable to sleep, he glowed between the sheets as he listened to the night sounds, muffled as if under a thick layer of cotton. They either thinned or thickened the following morning, and if thickening, there was no change the next day but a fluid and calm extension of the previous night.

His biggest fear was his fearlessness. Whole, no pains or wants or expectations. Not even the non-fear he felt, since not-working-out was the natural state of things, unchangeable, irreducible to any effort. Were he friendlier with the waters or the winds, he'd perhaps have better parameters for understanding the quiet gliding of fish, birds. Terrestrial creature that he was, another fear of his might be losing the ground under his feet. And fiery creature. The Great Absence crackled and sizzled inside him.

His invisibility didn't render him invisible, though: it carefully bound him to a particular body and a particular voice and certain habitual movements and personal gestures which apparently were really him. So it wasn't true they wouldn't see him. They would and they did see, yes, that shell that perfectly reproduced his outside. So perfectly indeed no one questioned when he took longer pauses between words, stared into space for too long, slowed down the gait of that false body. Behind the shell, however, the crystal glowed. Under the earth, will-o'-the-wisp buried so deep, his skin didn't even glisten.

Something he'd never have, and he was so conscious of this ever-present absence that, as paradoxical as it might seem, he felt whole in this state of lack. This only happened when he was in It, because once he was out, instead of smiling or doing things, he often cried bitterly, as if only pain could bring him back to that former stage. His unrelenting and inconsolable pain, in sobbing fits that made his whole body shake, each time his shell cracking a little more, breaking the frame, chipping the glass, putting out the fire.

It was a different kind of happiness, this leaving behind what was also happiness. Immersed, he wallowed in his emotions: he had violent desires, small cravings, dangerous urges, cloying tenderness, virulent hatred, insatiable lust. He listened to sad songs, drank to awaken drowsy ghosts, wrote or reread passionate letters, overflowing with roses and cliffs. Exhausted then, he would sometimes drown in a dreamless sleep, sometimes – when the general outline of his emotions was artificially provoked (but that one day, on another plane, the earthly one where he supposedly liked to walk, it would really happen) it wasn't enough – populated by cold reptiles, trying to wrap you in sticky tentacles, green eyes with vertical pupils.

He wouldn't know for sure how or when it happened. But one day – someday, any day, on a regular day – he realized something. No, he really wouldn't know how to say what he realized. But it was like this: looking at himself in the mirror, one morning, he noticed the light green reflection. It's back, he thought. And in that very instant, so immediately he nearly thought it was what was before, he sang, feeling like himself again. On the second verse, small contraction, he had again the glistening glass shard between his fingers. But before his fingers bled, he prepared a drink, though it was still morning, and drank it slowly, intently. Before swallowing the liquid, his body gained sudden new vortexes, framing a drawing of a face, quietly resting over a hand, eyes fixed in the distance.

That was a busy day. His shell cracked and mended itself again, gloomy evening and blinding morning interspersed. He smoked too much, without finishing a single cigarette. And he drank too much coffee, leaving some over at the bottom of the cup. He was hot-headed, absent-minded. During a break from his absence, he got distracted thinking of new names for it, in shock and fascination, the Great Indifference, or the Great Absence, or the Great Departure, or the Great, or The, Or. Out of understanding or maybe hope, who knows, that naming it also meant controlling it.

It didn't. He stopped caring. Taken by breaks of anonymity, he crossed the afternoon, stayed awake through the night, until he met morning again, and another afternoon, and another night still, and another morning, and so on. For years. Until his temples turned gray, until the wrinkles around his lips grew deeper. Had there been a moment of rest, he would have asked for help, though he didn't exactly know how, or from whom. And there wasn't. But because things tend to happen this way, perhaps because of magic, fate, signs, or simply chance, who knows, or maybe because it's natural that it was like this, and less than natural, inevitable, fatal, a tragic spell – anyway, on a certain day, one to remember, someone touched him lightly on the shoulder.

He looked to one side. On that side stood this Other Person. The Other Person looked at him with thoughtful brown eyes. The thoughtful brown eyes were warm, slightly worried, a bit too full of expectation. The transformations were so fast, at first he couldn't tell if the Other Person saw him or It, if the Other Person was addressing the frame, the shell, the glass, or if it was the drawing, the original body, the drops of blood. At first. Then in a second, he was absolutely sure he wasn't invisible anymore. The Other Person looked at something that wasn't a thing, but him. He looked at something that wasn't a thing, but the Other Person. His heart beat and beat, full of blood. Resting on his shoulder, the Other Person's hand was heavy with veins filled with blood, throbbing gently.

Something burst, shattered into pieces. From then on, everything became even more complicated. And real.

Sergeant Garcia

In memory of Luiza Felpuda

"Hermes!" The whip cracked against the worn wood of the table. Louder, almost shouting, almost angrily, he repeated: "I said Hermes. Which one of you is the dumbass?"

I stepped forward from the back of the room.

"It's me, Sir."

"*It's me, Sergeant.* Repeat."

The others stared, naked like me. All I could hear was the sound of the rusty fan blades spinning above, but I knew they were all laughing quietly, nudging each other in excitement. Behind him, the peeling plaster wall, the navy-blue window open to the courtyard full of cinnamon trees with the whitewashed trunks. Not a breeze in the motionless treetops. And the flies, sluggish from the heat, so dizzy they bumped into each other in midair, between the stench of warm horse shit and the men's dirty bodies. And suddenly, even more exposed than the others, me: in the middle of the room. Sweat dripped from my armpits.

"You deaf, dumbass?"

"No. No, Sir."

"No, Sergeant."

"No, Sergeant."

"Why didn't you answer when I called you?"

"I didn't hear you. I'm sorry, I..."

"I didn't hear you, Sergeant. Repeat."

"I didn't hear you, Sergeant."

It was almost funny, his cold green snake eyes almost completely covered by his brows, sharply angled above his nose. I was starting to hate that thick mustache, a hairy caterpillar crawling over his mouth, a black velvet curtain parted over his wet lips.

"Got wax in your ears, moron?"

He looked around, seeking approval, giving permission. Relief swept over the room. The men laughed freely now. To my right, I could see the German with the broken rib, the tip almost poking through his belly, shaking with toothless laughter. And the chunky black man's shriveled balls.

"No, Sergeant."

"And up your ass?"

The chorus of laughter staggered and stopped. The ceiling blades scraped the silence again, like in a Western movie, one second before the first shot. He looked at the men, one by one. The laughter resumed, raucous. The tip of the broken rib shook in the air, *an accident in der farm with meine sister.* The leaves at the top of the cinnamon trees still motionless. The shriveled balls, as if there were nothing inside them, *I'm a black belt, you feel me?* A fly fluttered next to my eye. I blinked.

"Forget it. And don't blink, knucklehead. Only if I say so."

He got up and walked toward me. The white t-shirt had large pit stains under his hairy arms, crossed over his chest, the tip of the short riding crop, tense and erect, tapping rhythmically on his close-cut hair, stiff with grease, glued to his skull. Out of nowhere, the whip came toward my face, veering less than ten inches away, whistling, to crack down on his boots. I shuddered. It was ridiculous, the feeling of having my ass exposed, pale and probably shaking, in front of half a dozen naked men. The caterpillar contracted, a slug sprinkled with salt, the curtain drawn to one side. A glint of gold danced over his left canine.

"You scared, princess?"

"No, Sergeant. It's that – "

The whip snapped on his boots again. Leather on leather. Dry. The whole room seemed to shudder with me. On the wall, the portrait of Marshal Castelo Branco trembled. The laughter stopped. But along with the whir of hot blood in my head, the rusty fan blades, and the heavy flight of the flies, I could also detect a nasty, disgusting panting. The others waited. I waited.

Was this what it was like for a Christian in the arena? I wondered without meaning to. The lion toying with his victim, lazy paws in the air, before the fatal blow.

"I do the talking around here, all right?"

"All right, Sir. Sergeant."

"Stick to *Yes, Sergeant* or *No, Sergeant*. All right?"

"Yes, Sergeant."

Very close, the smell of human and horse sweat, warm shit, alfalfa, cigarettes, and grease. Without moving my head, I could feel his snake eyes slowly traveling over my entire body. Bored lion, Spartan general, so focused he could find the scar from barbed wire hidden in my right thigh, the three stitches from a rock under my hair, the little marks, spots, even the ones I didn't recognize, all the warts and most secret moles on my skin. He moved his cigarette with his teeth. The hot ember almost touched my face. The nipple of his protruding chest brushed against my shoulder. I shuddered again.

"You real sensitive, huh? A nice little boy from a good family, huh? If you ever get in trouble, you'll see what's good for you."

The men shifted on their feet, restless. Romans, they wanted blood. The whip, the boots, the snap.

"At-ten-tion!"

I straightened my spine. My neck hurt, stiff. My hands seemed made just out of brittle bones, no flesh, skin, or muscles. He crushed his cigarette with the heel of his boot. He spat to one side.

"At ease!"

He turned quickly on his heels, heading back to the table. I crossed my hands behind my back, trying in vain to cover my bare ass. Beyond the tops of the cinnamon trees, the blue sky didn't have a single cloud. But down below, along the river, the horizon was starting to turn red. With an open palm, someone swatted a fly.

"Shut up, you idiots!"

He looked at my chest. And lowered his gaze a little more.

"So you're the one called Hermes?"

"Yes, Sergeant."

"You sure?"

"Yes, Sergeant."

"Where did you get a name like that?"

"I don't know, Sergeant."

He smiled. I sensed another attack coming. And I almost admired his ability to control the reactions of that herd of wild animals to which, as far as he was concerned, I must belong. Juicy prey, weak and vulnerable flesh. Like an idiot, I thought of Deborah Kerr surrounded by lions in CinemaScope, luxurious, white tunic, roses in her hands, an old picture in my grandmother's house, Cecília among the lions, or was it Jean Simmons? a figure from catechism, the-Christians-were-forced-to-renounce-their-faith-under-penalty-of-death, Father Lima ran away with the barber's daughter, who therefore must have turned into a headless mule, as the legend goes, the daughter, that is, not the priest or the barber.

The silence growing. A worn-out horse crossed the empty

space of the window, stage, screen, my mind galloped, Steve Reeves or Victor Mature, alone in the arena, sweaty chest, the martyr, strangling the lion, the corners of his mouth, no, that wasn't it, the-angles-of-his-lips-turned-downward-in-a-herculean-effort, the hero conquered the horned beast's beastliness. The fly landed right on the tip of my nose.

"Were you by chance raised in a barn?"

My face burned. He stubbed out his cigarette in the small helmet propped up with three crossed rifles. And looked at me straight in the eye for the first time, unwavering, sharp eyebrows over his nose, deep, a hawk watching its prey, fierce. The fly took off from my nose.

Don't hurt me, I thought with all my strength, I'm only seventeen, almost eighteen, I like to draw, on a wall in my room I have a Guardian Angel in a broken photo frame, the window opens to a jasmine bush, I get dizzy in the summer, Sergeant, I feel a kind of sweet nausea, all night, every night, all summer, sometimes I climb out the window naked with something I don't quite understand happening in my veins, then I open *One Thousand and One Nights* and try to read, Sergeant, *You are a dervish by profession and live a very quiet life, only caring to do good*, then in the morning my mother always says I have circles under my eyes, and knocks on the door when I'm in the bathroom and says again and again that the Nara Leão album is terrible, that I should stop drawing so much, because

I'm already seventeen, almost eighteen, and have nothing to show for, Sergeant, no friends, just this dry dizziness from having just started to live, so many things I don't understand, every morning, Sergeant, forever, amen.

Sparks darted like comets before my eyes. I was afraid I'd fall. But the highest leaves on the cinnamon tree began to move. The sun almost sinking into the Guaíba. And I don't know if it was because of the look in his eye, or because my nose was free of that fly, or my story, or that nice breeze coming from the river, or out of sheer exhaustion, but I stopped hating him in that moment. Like I'd changed radio stations. This one, I vaguely sensed, had no static.

"So, Mr. Hermes, you're the one with flat feet, heart palpitations, and low blood pressure? The doctor told me. And you're an only son, too? With a single mother?"

"Yes, Sergeant," I quickly lied, the doctor is a friend of my father's. Some doubt crossed my mind, what if he found out? But I was sure: he already knew. All along. Right from the start. I let go of my shoulders, lighter. I looked deep into the cold depths of his eyes.

"You work?"

"Yes, Sergeant," I lied again.

"Where?"

"In an office, Sergeant."

"You study?"

"Yes, Sergeant."

"What?"

"College prep, Sergeant."

"And what are you applying for? Engineering, law, medicine?"

"No, Sergeant."

"Dentistry? Agronomy? Veterinary science?"

"Philosophy, Sergeant."

An electric current ran through the others. I waited for him to attack again. Or laugh. He began examining me again, slowly. Respect, that look, or pity? His gaze paused, right below my navel. He lit another cigarette, Continental with no filter, I could see, the lighter shaped like a bullet. He looked out the window. He must have been looking at the red sky over the river, the orange of the sky, the almost purple color of the clouds stacked along the horizon of islands. He turned his eyes back to me. Pupils so dilated the green looked like smooth glass, easy to break.

"So, Mr. Philosopher, you're exempt from serving your country. Your certificate will be ready in three months. You can get dressed." He looked around, at the German, the black man, the other men. "And you, uncultured pigs, have some dignity and see if you can follow the boy's example. If it weren't enough that he provides for his single mother, he's going to be a philosopher one of these days, while you'll just keep grazing like cattle until you drop dead."

I walked to the door, so triumphant that my feet were like

leaves dancing in the wind in the late afternoon. They made way for me. Slow, defeated. Before walking into the other room, I heard the whip cracking against the black boot.

"At-ten-tion! You think this is your mother's house?"

2

Standing at the iron gate, I looked straight at the sun. My old trick: everything around so bright it became its opposite and turned dark, filling up with shadows and reflections that slowly came together, organized in the shape of objects or simply dancing freely in the space in front of me, without forming anything. Those were the ones that interested me, the ones that danced loose in the air, without becoming part of the clouds, the trees, or the houses. I didn't know where they went after my eyes readjusted to the light and put everything in their place again: house – walls, windows, and doors; trees – trunk, branches, and leaves; clouds – wisps or puffs, sometimes white, sometimes colorful. Each thing was each thing and whole, in the union of all its infinite parts. But the shadows and reflections, those that didn't join any shape, where were they kept? Where did the parts of things that didn't fit into themselves go? Deep into my eyes, waiting for them to be dazzled again? Or among the things that were really things, in the empty space between the end of one part and the beginning of another in a thing that's whole? Like behind reality, a spirit of darkness or light, chiaroscuro hidden in the innermost depth of a tree trunk or in the space between a brick and another or between two wisps of cloud, where? The cicadas hissed in the courtyard of whitewashed cinnamon trees.

I took a deep breath, lifting my shoulders to take in more air. My body had never seemed so new. I began to walk down the hill, leaving the barracks behind. The sun sank into the river like a suspended ball of fire. I shook the trunk of a manacá tree, and sweet-smelling petals rained down on my head. Around the first corner, the old Chevy pulled up beside me. Like a big gray bat.

"Headed to the city?"

Acting surprised, I peered inside. He was leaning out the window, the sun shining on his near-smile, making the gold filling in his left canine glint.

"You want a ride?"

"I'm taking the tram right over on Azenha."

"I can take you there," he said. And opened the car door.

I got in. His cigarette moved from one side to another in his mouth, while his hand shifted into first gear. The breeze coming through the window ruffled my hair. He held the cigarette, unfiltered Continental, I noticed, between his yellowed thumb and forefinger, spat out the window, then looked over at me.

"Were you scared of me?"

He wasn't a lion or a Spartan general anymore. His voice soft, he was now an ordinary man sitting at the wheel of his car. I pulled a pack of gum from my pocket and slowly unwrapped a piece, without offering him one. I chewed. The sugar coating broke apart, a cold burst opened up my throat. I sucked in the air so it would feel even colder.

"I don't know." And almost added *Sergeant* at the end. I smiled to myself. "Well, I was a little at first. Then I saw that you were on my side, Sir."

"No *sir*, please: Garcia, the whole gang just calls me Garcia. Luiz Garcia de Souza. Sergeant Garcia." He made a mock salute, then spat again, after taking the cigarette out of his mouth. "So, you thought I was on your side, huh?" I tried to say something, but he didn't let me. The car was reaching the bottom of the hill. "I saw right away that you weren't like the others." He looked at me. I wasn't cold or afraid, but I shrank in my seat. "I have to deal with stupid people all day long. I can't even tell you. So when a refined young man like you shows up, you take notice." He ran his fingers over his mustache. "So, you want to be a philosopher, huh? Tell me, what's your philosophy of life?"

"Of life?" I bit down harder on the gum, but the sugar was gone. "I don't know. The other day I was reading this guy, Leibniz, the one who came up with the monads, you've heard of him?"

"The what?"

"The monads. He's this guy who said that everything in the universe is... Like closed windows, or boxes. Monads, you know? Separate from one another." He furrowed his brows, curious. Or confused. I continued. "Incommunicable, you know?"

"But everything?"

"Yes, everything, I think. Houses, people, every one of them. Animals, plants, everything. Each one a monad. Closed off."

He stepped on the brake. I put my hands out in front of me.

"But do you really believe that?"

"I think so."

"Well, to tell you the truth, I don't really understand that stuff. I spend the whole day in those barracks, with all those morons, rougher than sandpaper. And you really gotta treat them like that, roughly, you gotta keep a tight hold on them, a short rein, or they'll ride you and life becomes a living hell. I don't have time to waste thinking about the universe. But I think it's nice." His voice softened, then hardened again. "My philosophy of life is simple: you walk over people before they walk all over you. None of that monodo stuff. But you still have a long road ahead of you, kid. You know how old I am?" He studied my face. I didn't say anything. "Well, I'm thirty-three. At your age, I was wandering around aimlessly, killing smugglers on the border. The army was what put me back on track, or I would have become a criminal. Life's taught me to be more open, accepting. Just can't stand Communists. But thank God the revolution's taken care of that problem. I've learned to look out for myself, Mr. Philosopher. To defend myself tooth and nail." He tossed out his cigarette. His voice was soft again. "But with you it's different."

I bit down even harder on the gum. Now it was just a tasteless paste.

"Different how?"

He looked right at me. Even though the wind was coming through the open window, something warm settled in the car, in the smoky air between us. There could be bridges between the monads, I thought. And bit the tip of my tongue.

"A fine young man, educated. Handsome." He made a quick turn. The tire squealed. "Listen, do you really have to go right now?"

"Not immediately, no. But if I get home really late my mom gets mad."

Two more blocks and we'd be at the tram stop, across the street from the Castelo movie theater. Quickly, I had to say or do something, I just didn't know what, my heart beat strangely, my palms were damp. I looked at him. He kept looking at me. The tiny houses of Azenha passed by, one on top of the other, spilling into each other, a pink wall, a blue window, a green door, a black cat in a white window, a woman with a yellow headscarf, calling to someone, the cemetery ridge, a girl jumping rope, the cypresses being left behind.

He reached out his hand. I thought he was going to shift gears, but his fingers moved past the stick and landed on my thigh.

"Listen, do you feel like going somewhere with me?"

"Where?" I was afraid my voice would crack. But it didn't.

Slow spider, his hand went a little further up, along my inner thigh. And he squeezed it, warm.

"This place I know. Real nice. We might be more comfortable there, you know how it is. No one would bother us there. Would you like to come?"

We had passed the tram stop. All the way down, where the river met the Guaíba, only the top half of the sun was emerging from the water. I always thought the sun must have been rising in Japan – antipodes, monads – at this hour. I had the feeling that the world was huge, full of unknown things. Neither good nor bad. Loose things like those reflections and shadows in the midst of others, as if others weren't there, just waiting for the moment when we'd be obfuscated, floating among what we could touch. Like: inside what we could touch, in hiding, was what was only visible when our eyes were so filled with light they could see the invisible, it became tangible. I didn't know the answer.

"Can I have a cigarette?" I asked. He lit it for me. I coughed. My father, his belt in hand, now you'll have to smoke this whole pack, you piece of shit, we didn't raise you like this. The warm hand moved up, pulled up my shirt, a finger went inside my belly button, squeezed it, joined the others, hairy spider, going back down, crawling between my legs.

"Of course you do. I can tell that's all you want right now, kid."

He held my hand, put it between his legs. I spread my fingers a little. Hard, tense, stiff. Almost bursting out of his green pants. It moved when I touched it, and swelled up even more. Porous-cavities-that-fill-with-blood-when-aroused. My cousin yelled at me: fag, faggot, niahniahniah. The wind disheveled the greenery of Redenção, the coconut trees along João Pessoa. Faggot, fag, niahni-ahniah. And no, I didn't know.

"I've never done this."

He seemed happy.

"Really? Never? Not even as a young boy? Fooling around down the river? Not even with women? Some hooker? I don't believe it. Not even with a horse? Big guy like you."

"It's true."

He slowed gears and leaned over me.

"I'll teach you, then. Would you like that?"

I took a deep breath. I suddenly felt dizzy. From inside the houses, the trees and the clouds, shadows and reflections were peeking at me, waiting for me to look into the sun again. But it had already sunk into the river. At night, the sparks of light slept quietly, out of sight, hidden in the middle of things. No one knew where they'd gone. Not even me.

"I would," I said.

3

I wished I could stop, but I couldn't control my legs, my head turning in all directions, as I walked up the hill behind him, you know how it is, he said, there's always people minding other people's business, it's better if I go first, wait by the blue gate, you come slowly, making like you've never seen me before. As if I'd never seen him before, I followed that green trail, my hands in my pockets, the cigarette between my lips, suddenly disappearing into the gate with a quick look back, a hook pulling me in. I dove into the shadow behind him. I climbed the cement steps, pushed the door open, old wood, cracked glass, entered the dark living room, which smelled of mold and stale cigarettes, wilted flowers resting in slimy water.

"The usual, then?" she asked, looking more closely I corrected myself in my head, he, in a colorful robe, quilted and covered in red stains, from tomatoes, lipstick, nail polish, or blood. "I see what you're up to, huh, Sergeant," she winked, playfully, at the sergeant and me.

"Is this your latest victim?"

"You know Isadora?"

Her damp hand, covered in rings, her long red nails, the polish chipping, like the door. I shook it. She laughed.

"Isadora, darling. You've never heard of her? Isadora Duncan, the dancer. Such an elegant woman, mar-velous, my idol, I like her so much I took her name. Can you imagine if I called myself Val-demir, the name my dear mother gave me? Poor thing, she meant well. But that name, oh, that name. So tacky. So I changed it. God willing, one day I'll die strangled by my own scarf. Is there anything fancier?"

"Cool," I said.

The sergeant laughed, rubbing his hands.

"Don't mind him, Isadora. He's a bit embarrassed, says this is his first time."

"Goodness. Such a big boy. And you've never done it, my dear? Never ever, really?" Her hand on my shoulder, a stone from a ring lightly scratching my neck. She rolled her eyes. "Tell Auntie Isadora the truth, the whole truth, nothing but the truth. You've really never done it, kid?" I tried to smile. The corner of my mouth quivered. She kept talking, her little eyes somewhat crossed, shadowed with blue. "Look, everything's going to be fine, you can relax. There's a first time for everything, right, it's a historic moment, darling. It even deserves a celebration. A little drink, Sergeant? I have some of that wonderful cachaça you like."

"The boy is in a hurry."

Isadora winked, mischievous, her eyelashes stiff with mascara, little black flakes sprinkled across her cheeks.

"In a hurry, huh? I see. It's not every day we have fresh meat on the table. Premium quality, right, Sergeant?" He laughed. She twirled the key in her hands and for a moment I thought of a baton twirler leading an Independence Day parade, tossing her baton with multicolored ribbons in the air. "All right, all right. I'll take you lovebirds to the bridal suite. How about room 7? Lucky number, right? After all, you only have one shot at your first time." She slipped past me into the dark hallway. I'm sure the boy will love it, become one of my regulars. No one forgets a woman like Isadora."

The sergeant pushed me forward. There I was, squeezed into that narrow hallway between the green uniform and the stained robe, sweat and sweet perfume. Isadora was singing, *que queres tu de mim que fazes junto a mim se tudo está perdido de amor?* A dry sound, metal against metal. The bed with dirty sheets, a roll of pink toilet paper on the crate that served as a bedside table. Isadora popped her uncombed head through the doorway.

"Have fun, kids. Just don't scream too loud, or you'll piss off the neighbors."

Her head disappeared. The door shut behind her. I sat on the bed, my hands in my pockets. He came very close. The bulge stretching his pants, right before my face. The smell: cigarette, sweat, horse shit. He stuck his hand through the collar of my shirt, slid his fingers down, pinched my nipple. I shuddered. From pleasure, disgust, or fear, I'm not sure. His eyes narrowed.

"Take off your clothes."

I tossed my clothes, piece by piece, on the dirty floor. I lay down on my back. Closed my eyes. They burned, as if I'd woken up too early in the morning. Then his heavy body fell on mine, and his wet mouth, a mouth deep like a well, a quick tongue licking my neck, going into my ear, coming into my mouth, a dry collision of teeth, metal against metal, while skilled fingers slid down my groin, invented a new path. *Então que culpa tenho eu se até o pranto que chorei se foi por ti não sei*, Isadora's voice said from far away, as if from deep inside a fish tank, Isadora drowned, her streaked makeup coloring the water, her shrill voice mixed with the moans, woven in with the warm breath, cigarette, sweat, horse shit, that now controlled my movements, turning me face down on the bed.

I smelled the sour sheets and wondered how many bodies had passed through them, and who were they. I held my breath. Eyes open, the coarse pattern of the fabric. With his knees, slowly, firmly, he opened the path between my thighs, seeking passage. Burning dagger, spike, sharpened spear. I tried to scream, but two hands covered my mouth. He pushed, moaning. I pictured a flashlight tearing open the darkness of a long-hidden cave, a secret cave. He bit the nape of my neck. With a sudden jerk, I tried to throw him out of me.

"You asshole," he groaned. "You dirty fag. You crazy little bitch."

I held the pillow with both hands, and with another jerk managed to roll onto my back again. His stubble scratched against my face. I heard Isadora's voice again, *que mais me podes dar que mais me tens a dar a marca de uma nova dor*. Wet and nervous, his tongue came into my ear again. His hands grabbed my waist. He pressed his entire body onto mine. I could feel the wet hairs on his chest making my skin damp. I wanted to push him off again, but between this thought and the action he only drew even closer to me, and then there was a deeper moan, and then his whole body shook, and then the warm, thick, viscous liquid spread over my belly. He relaxed his body. Like a sack of wet sand thrown on top of me.

I saw the yellow wood of the ceiling. The long cord, the light bulb hanging at the end of it. Dangling, unlit. That sweet smell floating in the gray shadows of the room.

When he reached out his hand for the roll of toilet paper, I slid my body along the edge of the bed, and suddenly was already in the middle of the room, slipping into my clothes, opening the door, glancing back in time to see him wipe his own belly with a piece of the paper, his green uniform on a chair, by his shiny black boots, and before he could return my gaze, I dove into the dark tunnel of the hallway, the deserted living room with its rotten flowers, Isadora's voice even more distant now, *se até o pranto que chorei se foi por ti não sei*, the clinking of glasses in the kitchen, chipped cups, peeling wood on the door, the four cement steps, the blue gate, someone yelling something, but far away, as far away as if I'd heard it from the window of a moving train, a shred of voice on the platform of a station that only gets farther and farther away, and me unable to piece together the words, like a foreign language, like a wet and nervous tongue quickly moving through the most secret part of me, only to awaken something that should never be awakened, that should never open its eyes or smell or taste or touch anything, something that should forever stay deaf and blind and mute in the innermost part of me, a hidden reflection, that would never see any light again, because it should remain caged and muzzled down in the swampy depths of me, like an animal in a stinking cage, between bars and rust, quiet tamed beast that's forgotten its own beastliness, forever and ever.

Though I knew that once awakened it would never go back to sleep.

I turned the corner, passed in front of the school, sat in the square as the lights were just starting to come on. The bare ass on the stone statue. Zeus, Zeus or Jupiter, I repeated. I went on: Pallas Athena or Minerva, Poseidon or Neptune, Hades or Pluto, Aphrodite or Venus, Hermes or Mercury. Hermes, I repeated, the messenger of the gods, thieving and androgynous. Nothing hurt. I didn't feel anything. Feeling my wrist with my fingers, I was aware of the beating of my heart. The air that went in and out, cleansing my lungs. Above the trees in the park, I could still see the reddish clouds, the pink turning purple, then gray, until the darker blue and black of the night. It'll rain tomorrow, I thought, it'll rain so hard it'll be as if the whole city were being cleansed. The gutters, the drains, the sewers, would take all the soot, all the mud, all the shit of every street to the river.

I wanted to dance on the flowerbeds, so full of a cursed joy people walking by would never understand. But I didn't feel anything. So it was, then. And no one knew me.

I hopped on the first tram, without waiting for it to fully stop, not knowing where it was headed. My path, I thought, confused, my path wouldn't fit along these tram tracks. I asked for passage, sat down, stretched my legs. Because no one forgets a woman like Isadora, I repeated without fully comprehending, leaning on the frame of the open window, watching the houses and greenness of Bonfim. I didn't know him. I'd never seen him in my entire life. Once awakened it will never go back to sleep.

The tram screeched as it turned the corner. Tomorrow, I finally decided, tomorrow I'll start to smoke.

Photographs

For Maria Adelaide Amaral

> *I'd like a photograph*
> *like this one – you see it? – like this one. [...]*
> *No… in the space we still have left*
> *put an empty chair.*
> —Cecília Meireles, "Encomenda" ["A Request"]

18 x 24: Gladys

I'm a hot blonde in my thirties, an 18:00-through-24:00 lady, as we used to say way back when, but I'd only whisper a phrase like that to myself, I've long learned that we give away our age in recollections like this, that's why I suppress the shock that floods my heart every time I randomly hear a song by Anísio Silva, Gregório Barros, Lucho Gatica, because besides being in my thirties and hot, I'm also modern and fun. The kind of blonde who stays till the end of and even after a cocktail party, and there are so many cocktail parties, and so many *after*-cocktail-parties in my life, I always say to the mirror, going down the generous, dangerous curves of the plentiful flesh God gave me with my carefully moisturized hands, with my extremely long fuchsia nails, and only God knows what it costs me to stay this firm and fresh. I'm a blonde coquette who loves cocktail parties, where I savor very sweet martinis with cherries, never with olives, I hate the bitterness, my mouth of secretly false teeth was made for tasting sweetness, every day, with my impeccable fuchsia nails, I repeatedly hit the keys on my IBM for efficient secretaries, my spine completely erect, highlighting the arrogant geography of my breasts, which in the old days earned me the coveted Miss Sweater sash, foregrounded even more by my tight shirts, which don't always show any cleavage, because little by little life has taught me that lust is less about full disclosure than about that fleeting sliver of flesh, barely glimpsed between the glove and the sleeve, and I have my own subtle reservations: I cross my legs, cunningly, so that the brief moment when my intimacy is almost completely revealed can be made of expectations rather than of cruel certainties. I was never a blonde who's too obvious, though I've always been confident, in a way, with my extensive knowledge of men, I very astutely realized that on the first meeting of the pupils you need to promise absolutely everything, but in the continuation of these stealthy rituals, I also know to hide behind frail whims and weak dismissals, in such a way that the more I dodge their advances, the more and more generously I promise, if you know what I mean – each *no* from between my shiny teeth stands for two, ten, two hundred *yeses, but not now*; I'd give you a tourmaline, but later I'll give you a trunk of diamonds. I'm a very easy blonde, and precisely for that reason extremely difficult, my truisms need complex maps, the countless x's pointing to the treasure's locations are mostly all made-up, mixed up with tangled jungles, muddy lakes infested with piranhas, hungry crocodiles, ravenous pygmies, tropical plagues, virulent fevers, invisible savageries, strychnine, and balm. But for a good hunter, and I've also learned the importance of letting the hunter see himself as the hunter even though he's actually the hunted, I, astute panther with sharp claws, feline gait, invisible ferocities, but as I was saying – I'm also a blonde moving through my own labyrinthine plots, so thick I often surprise myself as I go in the opposite direction of my previous route, a good hunter-hunted always knows how to get straight to the x, which isn't always remote, but only the more astute ones notice that the x can be, instead of hidden among countless dangers, on the edge of the gentlest of streams, in the shadow of the pinkest cherry blossom tree, in the freshest corner of the most fertile valley. For those, right away, for those, I open my satin thighs almost without hesitation, and I'm a guide experienced in all the steps that lead to the secrets of my honeyed cave, for those, I turn on the lights of my insides, I make it so the ominous shadows become soft penumbras, velvety tapestries carefully spread to soak in sweat and quench the thirst of valiant travelers, exhausted by the effort of keeping their tough firearms erect on the path through my intricate guts. It's true that sometimes I worry while I try to find the Great Conqueror, like America in her native virginal solitude, impatient for the Colombo that will show her to the world, exploiting her unto the last streak of gold to make her a captive slave, a servant humiliated by the cruelest colonialisms, and it's for that I get ready, for that I get polished and sculpt myself emerald – and I know it'll come. Two weeks ago, a gypsy tracked two spots, two loves between my heart line and the synthetic solitaire on my left ring finger, one already gone, she said, and right away I thought of that awkward scout who from time immemorial, confessable only under penalty of revealing a heart already marked by the human condition, I allowed to take his first tentative steps on my exuberant geography, and who after thirty-six months of practical learning I allowed to move on to other terrains, taking with him all the wisdom I'd granted him with tragic patience and lacerated joy, for I know that I am, delirious blonde, nothing more than the first, never the very last, never the one enthroned as a saint and mother of children, the chosen splendid and insatiable youthful womb. Wallowing in the abyssal melancholy of the crisis that followed, immersed in barbituric escapes, oceans of gin, nightly desperate phone calls, thirsty wanderings through the sinful alleys of pleasure, I solemnly swore at Oshun's feet to never be a parent to my protégés again, preparing them for existence only to fall into frantic abandonment. But the second one, the gypsy's nail scratched the line below my little finger, the second will appear in the next few months and, yes, he'll be the Great Conqueror, one so knowledgeable I'll have nothing to teach him, and myself so knowledgeable with all my training that I'll have nothing to learn from myself. We'll be, he and I, a tireless interchange of pleasure, the tinkling of sparkling crystals in a fervent and lustful champagne toast, tongues shared in voluptuousness, bodies enraged in the savagery of the wildest and mildest gestures, amid sweat, moans and robust, viscous fluids made of tropical waterfalls, seven falls, seven orgasms I'll have each time I plunge wrecked into his amazonic ejaculation. I wait for him, voracious nun, and since the gypsy drove me mad like this I've began to scrutinize the volume, the smells, the hair, of every man that dares come near this panther's lair, dreading that an extreme anxiety in the bottom of the brown twin moons of my eyes will show too big a thirst for your virile misogynies.

I carefully choose the tulle, the stones, the organdy, the earrings and shine, and it's so bright and devastating that I go face the dawn, despite the night's shadows, each new morning those who see me go out proud and apocalyptic, walking confidently in my heels, must think something like this: there goes a hot blonde in her thirties, on her way to meet her Great Conqueror.

3 x 4: Liége

I'm tan and thin, but not an island type, like Cecília wants, and there's also nothing Asian about me: I'm more on the British side, tan like a Brontë, any of the three. My little heart gestated in a coarse bog, I spend the winters trying in vain to find a path through the snow, which turns all paths into a single icy harborless mire, had I been born a hundred years ago, I'd wither away in white lace and scarlet hemoptysis, less from of an illness than out of refinement, unbearable to my eyes the steep cliff of the afternoon or the bright light of midday, shrouded by shadow which softened the harsh outline of living things, so I'd wither away, with a thin translucent hand reaching for the golden rim of the glasses over the leather cover of an old novel, full of impossible passions. In front of the mirror, I braid my long hair as an act of modesty, while the tips of my delicate fingers, nails cut to the quick, sometimes bitten, I gently touch the purple under my eyes, a token from a lonely sleepless night. Then I find a place by the window, rest my face on one hand and with the other I trace sad lines on the fogged-up glass, sometimes I write the names of places and people I'll never meet, faint sun behind weak clouds, sickly flowers, dim stars, brittle stalks, leafless trees, deep-set eyes, faces resting on thin hands like my own, I recognize them as my fingers trace and trace and trace the ineffable. About boys and mischief, I know almost nothing, my precarious knowledge of the flesh is limited to that cold goop a

Student left between my maidenly thighs one day, against a wall covered with the most insulting graffiti crudely scratched in with a nail, on a sepia autumn afternoon. Before the rules became clear, I was afraid he'd planted his coarse seed inside me, and every time I closed my eyes I could still smell his breath of beast in heat against my pale bosom, and feel the stones in the wall hurting my shoulder blades, my embarrassing run in ankle socks tripping over my patent leather shoes afterward, the countless baths and all the fragrances, all the perfumes, soaps, essential oils that I smeared on my body to rid myself of that flagrant animal stench. I prefer faint smells, gently withered roses, and in my most painful trances I always go and bathe the familiar corpses, cutting their hair and nails with infinite care, in a way, all my dead have also been my children, which I neatly polished so São Pedro wouldn't see one blemish when they knocked on heaven's door, so they'd have nothing against me in the kingdom of heaven when I arrive, which, I pray, will be very soon. But to this day the stench persists, though when my period comes I get inebriated like a madwoman with that blood, which assures the permanence of my purity, I let myself bleed for several hours, soaking my sheets and underwear, until I know for sure that not even a drop of that animal's vital liquid has tainted my guts: I reclaim them white like the linen of pillowcases, like the cotton of sheets, like the lace of these curtains that the wind blows against the violets outside, on afternoons when the sun takes its time to leave and the sky is painted purple. No, I don't pose any danger: I'm quiet like an autumn leaf forgotten between the pages of a book, defined and clear, an enamel pitcher and basin in the corner of a room – if handled with care, I pour out clear water over hands that will go on to refresh a face, but if handled by rude hands I shatter into the tiniest pieces, crumble into golden dust. I've been wondering whether I should leave undisguised the cracks from my many falls, of each time I was handled, and though I've tried I've come to learn that my tenderness is not enough to inspire softness in another, but still I insist – my gestures and words are frail like me, and so tawny that they barely appear in the dark, sketched with shading, I'm nearly invisible, my step is nearly inaudible like I'm always walking on carpet, undetectable, hands so gentle that my touch, if I touched someone, would be lighter than the afternoon breeze. To drink, besides a cup of tea with *une larme de lait*, I sometimes might accept a glass of wine, but it has to be white so I won't get dizzy, and it has to be dry, so it won't burn my throat too much with its heat, which, I'm afraid, could go beyond the limit imposed by my modesty, and to wear, besides white, I tolerate only gray and beige, rarely black, which is too dramatic for someone who seeks to blend into the background, and not to stand out, on occasion I dare to wear burgundy, the clotted blood of its shades pleases me, reminding me of pain forever stagnated, and I never tried any shade of blue, too bright for my severity. On the pages I type up as a secretary, my bosses have never caught a single mistake, no correction in the margins, not even a stronger or fainter touch here or there, I'm always precise, perfect black characters on the immaculate white, and that's all. I humbly take the compliments, I go to the restroom twice a day, just after I arrive and just before I leave, when there's no work I cross my arms over my flat chest and simply sit, I exist more deeply this way, when silent, or I quietly open a certain volume of lyric poems to savor some lines while I watch the busy street behind the windows. But since a gypsy read the faint lines on my palms two weeks ago, I've found little peace even in these moments of peace: two loves, she pointed, one already in the past, and with much bitterness I found the memory of that breathless Student, another one soon to come. Since then, I haven't really recognized myself. I take fewer trips to the restroom to wet my wrists and behind my ears, stimulating the circulation stuck in my veins, sometimes with the tap still on I'm struck by my own image, how I hate my own braids, the purple circles under my eyes, and everything that makes me like this, fleeting. I can barely contain my anxiety as I inspect every man who comes near me, at every corner I turn, on each bus I take, I look for him and I hate myself for this feverish restlessness, for the love I don't know yet and can barely conceive of, so deprived my life is of memories or measures. I struggle to paint light brushstrokes, I don't dare paint with oil or acrylics, only gouache and especially watercolors, where I search for the faint green of your complexion, and once in a while something is different and I surprise myself with my wildness, uncontrollable, playing with strong colors, flashy primary colors, rough shapes, sensual symbols, and that's when I dip into a cold bath in the middle of the night to cool down my contradictory flesh, feverish like Teresa of Ávila, shrouded in blankets, the words of a gypsy cradling me like a lullaby, I wonder if it might be the Lord himself who is approaching, and I don't recognize him. Each June, I know I won't be able to stand the following August, I hurt as I imagine that future gray afternoon when I'll meet him – not here, not in this muck, but in some other dimension of greater light, beyond my own body, a dumb twin trapped by his instincts, someplace discreet and contained, like the way I was for nearly three decades, which I frigidly overcame. I survive each morning by imagining I'm invisible to all who cross my path as I walk through doors and hallways that lead me to endless streets. No one guesses my secret, I sternly walk on the sidewalk, downward gaze so my thirst won't show: ah, I'm so tawny and thin no one will ever guess how I've been lately – chastely chiseled on top of a hill at wuthering heights, holding in my hands like a bouquet of blooming lilies an expectation so bright it's already certitude.

Pear, Grape, Apple

For Celso Curi

She is biting her nails when I open the door, her purse pressed tightly against her breasts. As usual, I think as she walks in, head down, and sits in her usual place, Mondays and Thursdays, five o'clock: as usual. I shut the door, walk over to the armchair in front of her, sit and cross my legs, making sure I pull up my pants first so they won't have those awful creases on my knees. I wait. She doesn't say anything. She seems to be staring at my socks. Slowly, I pull a cigarette out of the pack in my coat pocket, then tap it on the arm of the chair as I search for a lighter in my back pocket. Before lighting it, I think again that I should stop using plastic lighters, disposable. Someone told me they-are-nondegradable-and-I-should-care-more-about-the-environment. I can't remember who, when, where, or why. I play with the evil lighter between my fingers. Then I light the cigarette. She finally says:

"I'm sorry, but I think you're wearing mismatched socks."

Usually, a cigarette lasts from five to ten minutes. I try to spend as much time as possible on things like shutting the door, fixing my pants, thinking about lighters and eco-friendliness, so that she usually only gets to say something once I've finished my first cigarette. Almost always after I've asked very cautiously what she's thinking about. Only then she sighs, looks up, looks me in the eye. This time, however, she doesn't sigh. I consider telling her that I woke up too early, in the dark, and that... Instead, slowly, I ask:

"And does this bother you?"

She tenses her shoulders, and they go up almost to her ears. Then she releases them slowly, as if massaging herself.

"It's not that it bothers me, it's just – Look, honestly, I don't really care about your socks."

She lets out that last sentence quickly, as if she'd wanted to get rid of it, to see what I'd say. But I don't say anything. I limit myself to taking a drag on my cigarette, flicking away the ashes. I steady my glasses on my nose, these frames need to be readjusted, always sliding down. Ashes fall on my pants. I wet my index finger and thumb in order to remove them, throw them in the ashtray. She waits. I stare at her. She stares at me, then lowers her gaze. I keep waiting. I decide to help. Clipped:

"So you mean you don't really care about my socks?"

She opens her mouth.

"Isn't that what I said?"

She sighs. Uncrosses her legs, crosses her arms. Impatient:

"Yes, yes. But what I really mean is that today I don't feel like wasting. Not wasting, spending. Don't be offended. What happened is that... I'm not willing to spend... I – I bet on the plums."

Confused, I wait. She takes a cigarette out of her purse, searches in her bag, looking for a light. I hold out my nondegradable lighter, but she's already found a matchbox. She lights it, shakes the flame in the air. Confident:

"Listen, today I'm not willing to spend forty-five minutes discussing the sub- or un-conscious reasons why I said you're wearing mismatched socks, all right?"

I tap my cigarette against the lip of the ashtray.

"Something happened today."

I uncross my legs.

"Something very important."

I look at the clock. Fifteen minutes have gone by. I look at her again, waiting for her to talk. She doesn't, but keeps staring at me, her cheeks flushed, her eyes shining, as if she's sick with a fever. I wait a while longer. Now with my legs uncrossed, all I have to do is stretch them out to expose the color of the socks. I'm so curious about them, I move my leg forward just a tiny bit. Maybe the burgundy one with the white edge and the black and red plaid one. Ashes from my cigarette fall on my pants again, but a light shake is enough to make them fall off and onto the carpet. This time, I don't even need to wet my fingers to try to take them to the ashtray. When I look at her again her eyes are shining so much I decide to try to help her again. Calm:

"What is this very important thing that happened to you?"

She lowers her head, mumbles something, in a voice so soft I can't hear a single word.

"What was that?"

She puts out her cigarette. Anxious:

"On my way here I stumbled into a coffin. With a corpse."

If I move one of my legs very slowly to the right side of the chair and bend it at the knee, I can see the color of at least one of the socks. But she continues:

"When I turned the corner, a funeral procession was coming out of that big yellow house down the street." She takes another cigarette out of her bag. "No, that's not how it went. Before that I'd bought a kilo of plums." She holds two cigarettes in her hands for a moment, one lit and one not. Then she lights one with the other. "No, that's not how it went either. Before that, yesterday. I slept until three o'clock this afternoon. Then my mother asked me to come here."

She stops talking, makes a face. I don't know why, until she puts out the cigarette. She had lit the filter.

"Shit."

She's never said a bad word before, I think.

"Listen."

Maybe it's the green one, with gray diamond shapes. Along with the gray one with red details.

"I was on my way here. I was on my way and feeling dizzy, like

[124]

I always do when I sleep too much. And I don't even sleep, it just feels like I do. It was on one of those fruit stands that I saw them. I was walking with my head down, but... Such red plums. I was thinking about a lot of things when – "

"What things?"

"What things, what?"

"The ones you were thinking about."

She lights another cigarette. The right end, this time.

"I don't know, the things I've been. Very sad, or... Shitty, all of it. But that doesn't matter, please. Don't interrupt me right now. There's something inside me that keeps sleeping after I wake up, very distant. It was a long time ago." She takes a deep drag. And releases, almost forgetting to breathe. "That's when I saw the plums and they were so beautiful and so red that I asked for a kilo of them and that was the last of my money, you know, so I thought if I buy these plums I'll have to walk home but who cares that I'll have to walk home, might even loosen me up a little so I was eating the plums slowly, couldn't stop eating them, I'd already eaten about six of them when I turned the corner down the street, a coffin was coming out of the yellow house and I think the coffin was full, I mean, there was a corpse inside it because it was coming out of the house, not going in, and that was right when I turned the corner and there was no time to dodge it so I walked right into it and dropped the plums on the sidewalk, and it was then that I noticed these people in black with sunglasses and handkerchiefs and there were a whole bunch of flower wreaths, it must have been a very rich corpse and that hearse was parked there, and only then did I understand that it was a wake. I mean, a funeral. The wake is beforehand, right?"

"Right," I confirm. "The wake is before."

"They all stood there, staring at me. I knelt down and started to pick up the plums from the gutter. I wasn't worried that this was a funeral and it all had stopped because of me, you know? I picked them up one by one. Only after I'd put every single one back in the bag did things start to move again. I continued on my way here. They continued carrying the coffin to the funeral car. But first they stood there for a minute, like in a photo. Me picking up the plums and all of them staring at me. Are you listening? All of them staring at me, and me picking up the plums."

She stops talking for a moment. Then she repeats:

"Staring at me, all of them. Me, picking up the plums."

She puts out her cigarette. I check the clock. Fifteen more minutes to go. I light another cigarette. Touching the leather on the outside of her purse, she feels something inside it carefully. I assume she'll take out another cigarette but she doesn't even open the purse. Just feels this object inside it, distracted, with the tips of her fingers and bitten nails. So far away I have to bring her back.

"What are you thinking about?"

She laughs. She's never laughed before.

"There was this silly game we played when I was a girl. At

every house party, Cuba libre, you know." She takes the object out of her purse, but keeps it in her fist. "Such a long time since I last had a drink, since I last danced. God, so long since I've had any fun. You think people still party like that? And Cuba libres, do people still drink them? And that game, you think people still play it?" She looks at me. I imagine the object she's holding in her hand is a matchbox. "It was kind of a dirty game. But innocent dirty, kind of childish, I guess. You're blindfolded, then they point at someone else and ask if you want pear, grape, or apple. Pear is a handshake. Grape, a hug. Apple, a kiss on the mouth." She laughs again. "But we would find a way to talk to the person asking the questions and then, when they pointed at someone we have a crush on, we'd secretly take a peek. Then we'd say: apple." While she is speaking, I notice she is softly rubbing that object against her blouse, over her breasts. She laughs again: "That was the first time I French kissed."

Now her shoulders look too low, her back almost bent. Her eyes shine less, start to look misty. I think she'll cry. And what else, I think of asking. She straightens her posture.

"How much time do we have left?

I look at the clock.

"Five minutes."

"Five more minutes to go, no words anymore," she hums with a tone that strikes me as ironic. "There's a song like that, isn't there? Or I just made it up, who knows."

She continues rubbing the object against her blouse. What

might it be, I think without much interest. She looks at my socks again. Maybe one entirely white, the other blue with thin black stripes.

"Look, before I leave I'd like to say that I bet on the plums. That's what came to mind when I walked away. As I entered the building, facing away from the funeral procession, the entire time, without looking back, in the elevator, in the waiting room, as I came in and sat down here." Her eyes shine more. She's never looked me in the eye this much before. "I want to. I need to keep betting on the plums. I don't know if I should. I also don't know if I can, if it is... Allowed, I don't know. I think that I also don't know what possibility and obligation are, but I know very clearly what need is. Desire?" She interrupts herself as if I've asked a question. But I haven't said anything. "Desire, we make up."

She puts out her cigarette. And I yawn, unintentionally.

"Or not," she says, getting up. She's never gotten up before I say well, that's it for today, before.

I get up too, without having planned to. This has never happened to me before. She continues rubbing the object against her blouse. Only when she interrupts that motion, her hand stretched out to me, do I realize. It's a plum. Ripe. The color of red wine. Or blood, perhaps. She walks over to the table, places it on a book next to the phone.

"This is for you."

"Thank you," I say, unintentionally.

She fixes her hair with her long fingers before leaving.

"Happy New Year," she says, on her way out the door. Her eyes glimmer.

But it's just September, I think of saying. But only think of saying, because she's already shut the door behind her. I open it again, but the waiting room is empty. For a moment, I stand there, listening to the sound of the clock in counterpoint to the air conditioner. Then I walk over to the table. I touch the plum. The color of blood, of wine, seems to reflect itself on the polished surface of my nails. It's so glossy it shines: the peel almost bursting with the pressure from the stuffed pulp, which I picture as yellow, juicy, clicking against the teeth. I decide to call her parents, to advise them to have her committed again. But first I have to check the color of my socks. Maybe the lilac one with navy stitches. My glasses slide down my nose again. Or the yellow one with white stripes. There's no time left. The next patient knocks on the door.

Still Life

In memory of Orlando Bernardes

As you know, you'll say as if blindly groping in the dark, assuming previous knowledge, this might perhaps sweeten the other's heart a bit before you continue, but without a plan, though you've been planning for ages, you'll do things like turning on the lamp in the corner after turning off the brighter overhead lamp, making the mood in the room a bit more intimate, more welcoming, no tension in the air, even if you already know of the inevitability of your sweaty palms, of the excess of cigarettes or something like a light quiver that you hope won't show in your voice. But you'll say something like, for example, as you know, we humans unfortunately have this thing, emotions, but we contain ourselves, unfortunately. The other man might, ask why *unfortunately*? then you'll quickly say, so you won't stray too far from what you've established, anything like, it'd be so nice if we could have a relationship where neither of us expected anything at all, but *unfortunately*, you'll insist, unfortunately we, everyone, people, have – emotions. You'd ponder: people say things, and behind what they say there's what they feel, and behind what they feel there's what they are but don't always show. There are levels not fully formed, imperceptible layers, fantasies we can't always control, expectations that almost never are met, and above all, as you were saying, emotions. Which we don't always show. Because of this, unfortunately, you'll repeat it all, will insist on it, completely hopeless, and your only support will be the hand extended to you, which, you think with painful clarity, with every step, after each word, you'll be perhaps pushing away forever.

But I'm no longer capable of staying silent, you'll perhaps say, out of control and a bit more dramatic, because my silence is no longer an omission, but a lie. The other man will look at you blankly, not understanding that your rhythm follows the unfolding of an internal landscape that absolutely can't be put into words, sketched line by line in each minute of the many days and many nights of all those previous months, all the way back to that cursed or blessed night, you haven't dared to choose which one yet, when the magnetic circle of existence had for the first time, simply through banal or pure magic, intercepted the other man's circle.

In that silence that would follow, you think, you'll need to do something like put on a record or practice a gesture, but maybe you won't do anything, because the other man will keep looking at you with his empty eyes whose depths you plumb, scuba diver, for any minimal indication of some hidden treasure that might rise to the surface – a smile on your lips and your hands full of precious stones.

But in that silence that would certainly follow, you might also light a cigarette, and with your dry and tight lips, no smile, you'd avoid the dive so you won't run the risk of finding a sleeping beast.

Your heart will race, no one will hear it, and for a moment you'll maybe imagine that you could relax your limbs and simply touch him, which might magically light up the room with the light you've spotted in him as well, deep down it is so bright it's nearly palpable. Sharp light he cannot see, this other person seated next to you in the dim room, where outside sounds barely reach, as if you were both stuck inside a bubble of air, of time, of space, and again you'll pour a bit more wine in your glass so the liquid going down your trembling throat will meet this brightness you precariously try to turn into luminous words to offer him. You say nothing, and will say nothing, and, not exactly sure why, you'll blindly grope your way, your hands stretched out into the void, sensing the nothingness that you prepared yourself, meticulous and suicidal, through poorly woven silences and awkward words, poor thirsty thing, you hurt yourself, seeking water from someone else's well to quench your unwavering thirst.

Angels and demons would flutter colorfully around the room, but the butterfly catcher remains still, looking ahead, a lit cigarette in his right hand, a glass of wine in his left. The other man's presence would throb next to you, nearly bleeding, as if you'd stabbed him with your silent emotion. Your hands resting on fake crutches can't break the thick and invisible layer that separates you from him. For a moment you'll wish to turn on the light, let out a ridiculous laugh, end all of this, easy to pretend that all would be well, that there were never any emotions, that you didn't want to touch him, that you accept him as this throbbing distant friend, completely independent from your desire and all your amorphous feelings. In the following moment, so immediate it'll be born nearly at the same time as the previous one, delayed twin, you'll wish to put down the wine glass, put out the cigarette and offer your clean hands to this face that barely sees you, absorbed in contemplation of its own internal landscape.

But indifferent to his distance, almost violent, suddenly you want to violate with your mouth burning with alcohol and tobacco this other mouth in front of you. You wish to unveil inch by inch this body you've imagined for so long, with the language of a romance novel, until your tongue breaks through the barriers of fear and disgust, you continue, pulpy and impudent, until your voracious mouth has drunk all the liquids, your nostrils sucked every smell, and you've turned into one, alchemical, yours and his, together – lights off, a cliché from the movies, white garments glowing scattered across the floor.

And to desire him like this, with all the commonplaces of desire, this other man so close you sometimes think it unnecessary to say anything at all, because you mistakenly suppose you and him are one, he'll fill your body with new force, as if a powerful energy sprung from some distant center, long dormant, all the fairy-tale princesses parade through your head, who knows about this hidden light, and that's when you feel quite clearly that he is not you and you won't be him, this being, this other man, who magically or demonically, deliberately or casually, ignites in you such foolish youthful ardor, your soul a mirage, the delusion so strong you even are convinced that you have one. You want to ask him to simply be, to keep you in this tormented ecstatic state so you could also light him up with your touch, your tender tongue, the hard magic wand of your desire. But he knows nothing, won't even know if you stay like this, afraid that a clumsy word or gesture might puncture the dream, awaken you from your vivid synthetic emotion, disentangle you from the unknown inside him, the other man – who on the opposite end of the couch folds his hands over his knees, almost innocently, expecting, attentive and polite, for you to somehow finish what you started.

Much more than with love or any other twisted form of passion, you'll be surprised that he'll look at you now, because he knows nothing of his power over you, and in this exact moment you choose not to signal that you need him to light you up or extinguish you, waxing proud to deny him the knowledge of his strange power, so it won't bloody you between the nails now calmly resting on his knees, crossed at the ends of his fingers.

Ah, you will smoke too much, will drink in excess, will upset all your friends with your hopeless stories, night after sleepless night, the unbridled fantasy and fiery sex, you'll sleep through days, pass the nights, will miss work, will write letters you'll never send, will search for answers in cowrie-shells, numbers, cards, and stars, will think of an escape and suicide every minute of every new day, will helplessly cry until dawn in your empty bed, won't be able to smile or walk through the streets without seeing in someone else's gesture his exact gesture, in someone else's strange scent his precise scent.

He who will not suspect your ruin, flooded as you are now, on your side, as he contemplates that internal landscape of his where you don't even know where he keeps you, or if he does at all. In front of the mirror, on those sleepy mornings, you will trace with your fingertips the roots of new white hair on your temples, the rough, deeper paths in the dark valleys under your disenchanted eyes. You know everything about this potentially bitter future, and you also know that you can no longer turn back, that you're entirely subdued and your words, whatever they might be, will never contain enough wisdom to reveal if this door that will now open, as soon as everything has been said, will take you to heaven or hell. But you certainly know, with a certain touch of sweet self-pity, for all, that everything will pass one day, perhaps as quickly as it started, or slowly, it doesn't matter. Behind all the artifice, the only thing you'll never grasp is that in this moment you possess the unbearable beauty of something entirely alive. Like a trapeze artist who only notices the absence of the net after the jump, you turn on the lamp in the corner after turning off the glaring overhead light.

Music Box

In memory of Rachel Rosemberg

It was like her head was plunged under water, and an organ grinder was playing by the river. Little bubbles of sound softly burst against her ears, note after note, until she felt inside her a remote and slow melody that seemed to come more from the edge, from down at the bottom. Where perhaps there were green siltstones, colorful fish, shells, strange tangled plants. Moving her limbs to the sound of the notes, she tried to dive toward the white sand at the bottom. She knew where each movement came from: they sprang up from her center as if awakened by the musical notes, melodies and movement radiating through her muscles, dispersing unhurriedly along her skin until they reached her fingertips, which now fluttered, opening and lightly hitting the surface of the water before going in. But instead of sinking, little fish, she was suddenly lifted up, out, to shadows wrapped in outlines where she could vaguely make out something like the back of a large man.

Sitting on the edge of the bed, floating, in the dark, he slowly turned the crank of a music box.

She didn't say anything, just watched him mindlessly turn the crank over and over, sometimes faster, other times slower, making time speed up, notes suddenly lumped together, or unfurling like a cloud blown by the wind. Colored lint scattered in every direction, shadows growing sharper in the dark room. Lost in the corners, they faintly glowed before disappearing so slowly and lightly that if she wanted she could close her eyes and sink again.

Maybe mermaids, lichens, corals, nacre caves. With much effort, she rubbed her eyelids. And gently, only after he played the song in the music box so many times, over and over again, as if not to break a difficult spell, she finally rested her back against the headboard and asked in a low voice what had happened.

He was a large man, a quiet, shirtless man sitting on the edge of the bed. Curved back, low head. In his hands, the little box so tiny she couldn't actually see it. For what seemed like forever, she thought, the man suddenly a stranger, still like a painting, an enormous mannequin, a sculpture of salt or plaster, his large back so white it nearly glowed in the darkness of the room. He stopped playing it. She could tell because of the silence growing between the notes, less so than by the movement of his arm. The numbers on the digital clock shone next to her, bright red, so close all she had to do was turn her head to see the time. But she didn't want to know it, she didn't move. She almost extended her arm to touch him, but contained herself in time, drawing back her fingers in the air. There was no time, she repeated to herself without fully understanding it, there was no hour, there was no noise, there was no gesture. As if she were peeking through her own bedroom window from the outside, she saw a man sitting on the edge of the bed and a woman lying there, her head up, tense, very still, forever waiting for something that didn't happen.

"Was it a nightmare?" she asked then, but too abruptly, she noticed, her voice coarse, husky with sleep. And she reached for the bedside table and grabbed the pack of cigarettes, as if that would fix it.

"Want a smoke?" she offered, though she knew this communicated something more like "don't stress over nothing, my dear, it's the middle of the night, have a smoke and relax, I'm here, you can talk to me," establishing the rules of a game where there wouldn't be either a winner or loser, only the final gentle failure lovingly shared and agreed upon by both parties. Absolutely hidden in the middle of the room, the building, the city, the country, the continent, the hemisphere, the planet. At the center of the immense night of the universe. Forever, she shivered.

She remained silent. Almost angrily, she lit a cigarette with a dry click of the plastic lighter, and tossed it next to him along with the pack of cigarettes. She knew that as she inhaled her cigarette she was also communicating something like "alright, if you don't want my help you're on your own, my dear, I'll just smoke my cigarette over here and wait for either one of us to give up, and if you get tired first, you'll talk, and if I get tired first, I'll go to sleep one more time and tomorrow we'll wake up and have breakfast like every morning, my dear, and we'll never talk about this again, all right?" She grabbed the ashtray on the radio and quickly tapped her cigarette. Now, besides the red digits, the bright red tip of her cigarette also glowed in the dark. Even when she said nothing, it was always like she'd said something. And now it was so late that the sound of any car outside pierced through the silence. Please, she nearly asked, please, keep playing it. Quietly, she twirled her cigarette in the dark until the ember met the beginning of the circle of fire at the end of each movement. When she stopped, she noticed: he'd shifted in his seat and was staring at her.

"A tree," he said.

"What?"

"A tree, I saw a tree."

"You had a dream," she leaned over a bit more, as if to reach him or to somehow show him with her body that she was paying attention. But that didn't seem to matter to him. He talked without looking at her, looking through her and beyond the headboard, the wall, the empty space of the twelfth or thirteenth floor.

"What does it matter?" He placed the music box next to the pack of cigarettes and the lighter. The crank grazed the plastic packaging, producing a sudden note that echoed in the air. "What does it matter if I dreamt it, if I saw it, if it was today or tomorrow?

If I didn't even see it but only imagined it, what does it matter? I woke up thinking about this tree."

He spoke slowly, with no irritation. But he raised his hand with determination when she moved her body forward, as if to interrupt her before she even opened her mouth to speak. "Still," she asked, stubbing out her cigarette. "What kind of tree was it?"

"It wasn't just one, but two. Just wait and I'll tell you. Do you want to hear it?"

She quickly nodded yes. Without seeing his face properly, she noticed he was smiling, perhaps sarcastic. Or bitter, or sad, or simply distant, she understood it better now, as she hunched against the headboard. And this perhaps looked like respect, or submission, or interest, because he started telling the story.

"At first, I thought it was only one tree. I saw it from far away, I was walking and there it was, covered in flowers, lots of flowers of all colors, but I think especially purple and yellow, with some fallen on the ground. It didn't look real, it looked like a drawing, kind of like a painting, an illustration in a children's book, a Walt Disney movie. You know *Snow White*?" She smiled too, reassured, crossing her arms over her breasts. He didn't notice.

"A tree right out of a fantasy. The most beautiful I'd ever seen in my life. Then I stopped and stared at it. There was something there pulling me yet I couldn't move forward, I must have hesitated for a long time before I came closer, step by step, and suddenly

I was inside it. No, wait, it wasn't like that. Between the branches covered with flowers there was a kind of gap, an opening, a door, and I went through it until I was fully inside that colorful thing. It was dark inside it. It was full of tangled and tortured branches, and very dark, and very humid, it felt like a great pain had grown there in that hollow full of rotten leaves and withered flowers on the ground. Through the gap, the opening, the door, I could see the sun outside. But that place was far from the sun. It was something, something full of despair and gore, you know what I mean? So I thought of leaving immediately, without looking back, but at the same time I also wanted to stay there forever, and if I wasn't careful, if any part of me lost control, I would crouch down there on that cold earth, looking at the branches so twisted not even a sliver of sunlight from outside would ever pass through. I left, I didn't want to look back, but I did without even realizing it and there it was again just like the first time I saw it.

An enchanted tree, one of those you can make a wish to and maybe enter a special state underneath it and see, how do you say it, what is it again? the devas, right, the devas, the nymphs, the fauns. From the outside, from where I was, it was that sort of tree, like a beautiful deva that I almost saw, purple and yellow like the flowers, sort of dancing, perhaps playing the flute around it.

Then I remembered the dark and thought I understood it, and sort of by accident I came up with something more or less like this: it's from that tangled mess of pain and cold anguish and loneliness that it takes the beauty it gives out." He looked very tired when he finished the story and asked: "Do you know what I mean?"

"Was it there?" she asked tactlessly. He didn't answer. She reached for the pack of cigarettes, lit another one that she inhaled in a rage. She passed it to her left hand and extended her right hand to him with her right, digging her nails into his arm. "Was it there?" she repeated. "I need to know. Tell me, was it there, at that place? God, you haven't forgotten that damn place yet?"

As if he hadn't heard this, he gently touched the nails digging into his arm with his large and quiet hand.

"Do you know what I mean?"

She released the pressure.

"I do, of course I do." She brought her hand back, lowered her voice. "It's a beautiful story. And so… symbolic, isn't it?" She sighed, exhausted. "Is that how you feel? I get it, of course I know it all too well, better than you could imagine. Much better, my dear." She slowly ran her fingers over the curly hair on his chest. If there were more light, she'd be able to see the hair growing white toward his navel, and perhaps even feel what she usually did: that familiar sympathy, full of emotion, similar to something they'd once said was called *affection*, *tenderness*, *love*, something like that. But in the dark, as she felt his soft and delicate hair giving in to the pressure of her fingertips like she did now: she felt nothing.

A dryness like that of the cigarette she inhaled again, irritating her throat. She coughed.

"But it's not over," he said.

"What?"

"It's not over, the story is not over yet."

She noticed that he was smiling. But there was no sadness or irony in his smile anymore. Something denser, she detected. And took her hand off his chest as she realized it. It was a quiet and wicked smile, at the corner of his mouth, clenched teeth out of view. He was very close now, fully there, between her body and the bedroom door that led to the hallway and living room, suddenly so deserted no one would hear them if they screamed. But they wouldn't scream, she comforted herself, that it's been so long, that they've lived through so much together, no, no they wouldn't scream. He continued:

"I went back the next day. I was cold, I couldn't feel anything, I didn't have that fear of being inside the tree anymore or of that spell of being outside it, you know? So I walked around it looking closely, until I noticed there were two trees. You know those trees that usually grow by the river? That drooping one, with branches all the way to the ground, a big tree that looks tired and sad."

"A willow," she said. "Weeping." And relaxed her shoulders, almost light.

"Right. A willow, weeping. The other one, the one full of flowers was a bougainvillea. Then I remembered some verses you liked to recite, a long time ago. What were the verses again, about bougainvillea, and dying, and being born again? What were they, do you remember?" he asked, suddenly anxious and a bit childish, pulling at her foot the way he did on Sunday mornings, when she took too long to wake up and he would sing made-up tunes in the style of a music box: *Come see the sun oh my love! put on your skirt, let's go swim! the day is beautiful oh my love! today is Sunday, bright and sunny.*

A warm wave like a kind of joy rose up from her feet all the way to where he touched her face, making her chest rise as she said:

"Cecília Meireles, it was Cecília Meireles, it was that poem: 'Take me anywhere you'd like! I've learned from the bougainvilleas to let myself be pruned! and to always return whole.'"

He put out his cigarette. Then clapped his hands like a child:

"So beautiful, so beautiful. How does it go again?" And they recited it together, like a teacher who is serious and a bit old and patient and vaguely in love with a naughty student. "'Take me anywhere you'd like! I've learned from the bougainvilleas to let myself be pruned! and to always return whole.'"

"It's a love story," he whispered in her ear. "The willow and the bougainvillea, it's a beautiful love story between two plants."

She crossed her hands over his back, that big back of a large man, that good smell of cleanliness she'd known so intimately, for so long. And while he slowly brushed his shifting and wet mouth over her neck, she gently opened her legs, rotating her pelvis like in a belly dance, until she felt the bulge of his sex growing stiff under her belly. She moved her hand down to his waist, to tuck it under the thin fabric of his pajamas, stroking the ass that moved over her.

And she also licked his big manly ears so deeply and for so long, intensifying her movements until his member was so hard that it slipped out of his pajamas to rub, hot, her stomach.

"Come here," she asked. "My crazy boy."

But he got up so abruptly that the absence of his weight made her feel a kind of dizziness.

"No," he said. And he backed away again to the edge of the bed. I haven't finished the story yet."

"Oh my god, not that damned tree again."

"That damned tree," he repeated slowly.

"Still?" she tried to laugh, but he was distant again. One thing had suddenly turned into another, and she only noticed this shift after talking like nothing had changed, she only knew how to behave in the past, not in the present, still unknown. "So tell me," she asked, somehow knowing that it wasn't like that, that it wasn't like that anymore, that somehow it would never be like that. She crossed her arms as if talking to a child. "But tell it quickly."

"Real quick, don't worry. The next day, the third day, I went back again. It was the last time I went. I don't need to go there anymore. This last time I saw everything. I discovered the truth."

"So?" she asked. "What was it?"

The man grabbed the music box and held it between his hands, like he was going to play it. With the faint morning sun lighting up his face, she could now see his eyes were wide open, fixed on something she couldn't see, his face scruffy, his hand frozen in the air, and the gray hair on his chest. And she still felt nothing, except for the warmth stirring between her thighs.

He didn't say anything.

"What did you find out?"

He smiled without moving a single muscle on his face. Only the corners of his mouth quickly went upward, as if someone had pressed a button or pulled a hidden string. He turned the little box in his hands.

"I found out that it wasn't a love story. The willow was dry, dead. The bougainvillea had killed it. It wasn't a love story. She strangled him, took everything from him, killed him. That darkness inside was his weakness, his failure, his death. Do you understand what I'm saying? I'll speak very slowly so you'll understand: that frenzy of flowers and colors outside was her triumph. The triumph of her vanity at the expense of his life. An insane triumph, are you listening?"

As if she were very cold, she abruptly hugged herself. Unwittingly, she looked over and saw the clock.

It was five fifteen in the morning. He repeated:

"An insane triumph, a sick triumph. It wasn't love. It was loneliness and madness, rot and death, not a love story. Love has nothing to do with this. She was a parasite. She killed him because she was a parasite. Because she couldn't live alone. She sucked him dry like a vampire, to the last drop, so she could show the world those purple and yellow flowers. Those dirty flowers. Those disgusting flowers. Love doesn't kill. It doesn't destroy, it's not like that. That's something else. That's hate."

Very calm and quite casual, lighting another cigarette, pushing away a lock of hair that fell on her forehead, slightly cold, slightly sweaty, but nothing serious, the woman slowly raised her left eyebrow, a very characteristic gesture, a frequent gesture, habitual and not new, which she often used when she went shopping, asking about the price, as she drank from a cup of tea, or gave orders to her maid as she turned on the television, and asked absolutely calmly, absolutely in control, absolutely sure of herself:

"Are you trying to say you think I destroyed you?"

Putting down the music box very carefully, he said something in a voice so low she couldn't make it out.

"What?"

She didn't hear the answer. His two big and strong manly hands closed around her throat, tight and precise. The woman stretched her leg as if kicking the air, knocking over the music box. The sun had nearly come up when a note from a broken string resonated sharply in the air. Between the sound and the light, she could still see his manly smile all lit up, and if she could speak she'd tell him exactly how she felt: like her head was plunged under water, and an organ grinder was playing by the river.

The Day Jupiter Met Saturn
(Another Colorful Story)

For Valdir Zwetsch
and Maria Rosa Fonseca

"Everyone, mirrored stars
reflection of radiance"
—Caetano Veloso, "Gente" ["People"]

He was the first person she saw as she walked in. So handsome she lowered her eyes, wanting but not wanting him to notice her too. Someone handed her a plastic cup with vodka, ice, and a lime twist. She ground the peel between her teeth, stirring the ice with the tip of her index finger, not drinking. With activity around her, people getting up all the time to dance to loud rock music or disappearing into bedrooms to snort lines and smoke joints, she slowly managed to get to a rattan chair by the window. The clear night outside stretched over Rua Henrique Schaumann, the avenue of cheap Conga shoes & ponchos, she chuckled to herself. She chuckled to herself almost all the time, a thin young woman trying to control her own madness, subtly unhappy. She wet her lips with vodka, gathering courage to look at him again, a suntanned young man in white pants with unhemmed cuffs. She lowered her gaze again, though her skin was also tan, and sighed, letting go of her shoulders, her tense back pressed against the rattan of the chair. Just because it was a Saturday and she wouldn't, not this time, sit motionless by the stereo, the TV, the book, watching the phone not ring. She smiled as she looked around, well done, congratulations, here we are.

It's not that she was sad, more that she couldn't feel anything anymore.

Slowly, so as not to call too much attention to herself, she shifted in her seat, propping her elbow on the windowsill. She rested her face on the palm of her hand and her sleek hair fell over her face. She raised her head to get it out of her eyes, and then she saw the sky. A sky much brighter than the usual São Paulo sky, with the moon nearly full and Jupiter and Saturn very close. From this angle, she looked less like a living woman than a watercolor painting, frozen as if she were very calm, and in fact she was, only she couldn't feel anything anymore, she hadn't for a long while. Maybe because she didn't pose any threat sitting still like this, distant, the young man in the white pants made his way to her without her noticing. Him standing still next to her, seen from inside, a painting – but seen from outside, from the windows of the cars on their way to bars on the avenue, Chinese shadow carved against the red light.

And suddenly the loud rock music was over and John Lennon's voice sang *every day, every way is getting better and better*. In her head, a gun went off, five times. The woman's suddenly hardened eyes moved inside and met the man's suddenly hardened eyes. The memories they each kept, and there were so many, showed in their eyes so clearly she immediately understood it when he tapped her on the shoulder.

"Do you like stars?"

"I do. You too?"

"Yeah. You're looking at the moon?"

"Almost full. In Virgo."

"And Jupiter in conjunction tomorrow."

"With Saturn as well."

"Is that good?"

"I'm not sure. It must be."

"It is. Nice to run into you."

"Same here."

(*Silence*)

"Do you like Jupiter?"

"I do. I actually 'wish I could live on Jupiter where the souls are pure and the sex is new.'"

"What's that?"

"A poem by a guy who'll die soon."

"How do you know?"

"In February. He'll kill himself in February."

"Huh?"

(*Silence*)

"You got a cigarette?"

"I'm trying to quit."

"Me too. Just wanted to hold something in my hands right now."

"You already have something in your hands right now."

"Me?"

"Me."

(*Silence*)

"How do you know?"

"What?"

"That this guy will kill himself?"

"I know a lot of things. Some haven't even happened yet."

"I don't know anything."

"I can teach how to know, though not how to feel. I don't feel anything, haven't for a long while."

"I only feel, but don't know what the feeling is. When I do, I don't understand it."

"No one understands it."

"Sometimes you do. I can teach you."

"Unlikely, I died in December. Five gunshots in the back. You too."

"Me too, then I left my body. Have you left your body yet?"

(*Silence*)

"Do you take anything?"

"What?"

"Cocaine, codeine, morphine, mescaline, heroin, psilocybin, Ritalin, methamphetamine."

"No, nothing. Not anymore."

"Me neither. I've already taken everything."

"Everything?"

"Shrooms are a deal with the devil."

"Opium perfects reality."

"Now I want to get clean. In body and soul. I don't want to leave this body."

(*Silence*)

"I think I'm coming back. I used to wear colorful skirts, flowers in my hair."

"My braids went all the way down to my waist. Bangles covered my arms."

"Something got lost."

"Where did we go? Where did we stay?"

"Something found itself."

"And those rattles?"

"Those ribbons?"

"The sun is gone."

"The road got darker. But we know where we're going."

"Yes. Which way is north?"

"Find the Southern Cross. Then walk in the opposite direction."

(*Silence*)

"Are you a Virgo?"

"Yeah. And you, a Capricorn?"

"Yeah. I knew it."

"I knew it too."

"We're a good match: earth."

"Yes, a good match."

(*Silence*)

"Tomorrow I leave for Paris."

"Tomorrow I leave for Natal."

"I'll send you a postcard from over there."

"I'll send you a postcard from over there."

"My card will have a rock hovering over the sea."

"Mine won't have a rock, just the sea. And a palm tree peeking out in the corner."

(*Silence*)

"I'll drink ayahuasca and see you, Egyptian. By my side, looking at me from the corner of your eye."

"I'll drink devil's weed tea and see you, Tuareg. Lost in the desert, standing against the sun."

"Are we going to see each other?"

"In your tea. In my tea."

(*Silence*)

"When nights arrive early and snow covers all the streets, I'll spend a day in bed thinking of sleeping with you."

"When it's so hot I feel sluggish, I'll slowly sway in a hammock thinking of sleeping with you."

"I'll write you a letter that I won't send."

"I'll try to recompose your face from memory and I'll fail."

"I'll see Jupiter and think of you."

"I'll see Saturn and think of you."

"Twenty years from now they'll meet again."

"Time doesn't exist."

"Time does exist, and it devours."

"I'll look for your scent in another woman's body. And fail, because I'll have long forgotten it. Lavender?"

"Rosemary. When I look at the immense night from the Equator, I'll wonder if this was a hello or a goodbye."

"And what word or gesture, yours or mine, would be enough to change our paths."

(*Silence*)

"But that would be unnatural."

"Natural is people meeting and losing each other."

"Parallel lines meet at infinity."

"Infinity is endless. Infinity is never."

"Or forever."

(*Silence*)

"This is all too abstract. 'Kiss, Kiss, Kiss' is playing. Why don't you ask me to sleep with you?"

"Do you want to sleep with me?"

"No."

"Because it isn't not necessary?"

"Because it isn't not necessary."

(*Silence*)

"Kiss me."

"I'll kiss you."

She was the last person he saw as he walked out. So pretty he lowered his eyes, not knowing if she noticed him too. He took the elevator to the bottom floor, car keys in hand. He twiddled a key between his fingers, then softly bit the metallic end, bitter. His eyes fixed on the floors passing by, not paying attention to the people blowing their noses or putting in eyedrops. Slowly, he managed to get to a space by the door. Filtered party sounds and nighttime demands in the other apartments, dance at a glance, he chuckled to himself. He chuckled to himself almost all the time, a suntanned young man in white pants with unhemmed cuffs, trying to control his own madness, subtly unhappy. He bit his nail next to the key, thinking of her, a thin young woman with sleek hair sitting by the window. He lowered his gaze again, though he was thin as well. And sighed, letting go of his tense shoulders, unsteady feet pressing on the unstable ground of the elevator. Just because it was a Saturday, and because he was leaving, because he had yet to pack and the phone wouldn't stop ringing. He smiled as he looked around.

It's not that he was sad, just that he couldn't understand what he felt.

Slowly, so as not to call too much attention to himself, he pressed his right hand against the open elevator door and crossed the cold lobby, walking out to the street. He leaned against the lamppost on the corner, the wind blowing his hair, and then he raised his head to avoid it and saw the sky. A sky much brighter than the usual São Paulo sky, with the moon nearly full and Jupiter and Saturn very close. From this angle, he looked less like a living man than an oil painting by Gregório Gruber, his shape so clear it stood out against the avenue in the background, and in fact he'd been unable to understand anything, for a long while. Maybe because he didn't pose any threat, the woman leaned on the window up there and shouted something he didn't hear. From far away like this, the woman visible only from the waist up, she looked like a puppet, controlled by a concealed hand, the man by the lamppost shaking his head, a marionette, controlled by a concealed hand.

Suddenly, a car halted behind him, the radio blaring "By God's will, one day I might fly." In his head, a gun went off, five times. From where he stood, he couldn't see the woman's eyes. From where she sat, she couldn't see his eyes. But the memories they each kept were so many that he immediately understood and accepted this, as she disappeared from the window at the exact moment he crossed Rua Henrique Schaumann without ever looking back.

Those Two

In memory of Rofran Fernandes

I announce adhesiveness – I say it shall be limitless, unloosen'd;
I say you shall yet find the friend you were looking for.
—Walt Whitman, "So Long!"

1

The truth is, there was no one else around. Months later, not at first,
one of them would say that the office was a "desert of souls." The
other one agreed, smiling, proud that he wasn't included in that de-
scription. And little by little, between beers, they came to share sour
stories about unloved and hungry women, then soccer banter, Secret
Santa wish lists, fortune tellers' addresses, a bookie, *jogo do bicho*,
cards for the punch clock, the occasional pastry after work, cheap
champagne in plastic cups. In a desert of souls that were themselves
deserts, one special soul immediately recognizes another – maybe for
that reason, who knows? But neither of them wondered.

They never used words like "special," "different," nothing like that. Even though, without effort, they'd recognized each other the moment they met. It's just that neither of them was prepared to give a name to their emotions, much less to understand them. Not because they were too young, or uneducated, or a bit stupid. Raul was just a year over thirty; Saul, a year under. But the differences between them were not limited to these years, to these words. Raul was coming from a failed marriage, three years and no children. Saul, from an engagement so endless that one day it ended, and a derailed architecture degree. Maybe that was why he drew. Just faces, with huge eyes, no irises or pupils. Raul listened to music and sometimes, when drunk, he'd pick up the guitar and sing his favorite old boleros in Spanish. And movies, they both liked them.

They'd taken the same entrance exams for the same government office, but that wasn't when they met. They were introduced their first day at work. They said, pleased to meet you, Raul, pleased to meet you, Saul, then what's your name again? smiling at the same time at the coincidence. But discreetly, because they were new at the office and we never know, after all, where we stand. They decided right away that it was best to keep their distance, thinking they should only say the customary hello, how are you or, at the most, on Fridays, a cordial have a good weekend, then. But from the very beginning something – fate, celestial bodies, luck, who knows? – conspired against (or, why not, in favor of) those two.

Their desks stood next to each other. Nine hours a day, minus one for lunch. And lost in the middle of what Raul (or was it Saul?) would months later call "a desert of souls," so they wouldn't feel so cold, so thirsty, or simply because they were human, which didn't excuse them – or, rather, excused them fully and deeply, in the end: what else was there for those two but, little by little, to grow close, to really get to know one another, to get entangled? So that's what happened, so slowly they barely noticed it.

2

They were a pair of loners. Raul came from the north, Saul from the south. In that city, everyone came from the north, the south, the middle, the east – meaning that this trivial detail didn't exactly set them apart. But in the desert around them, everyone else had a point of reference, a wife, an uncle, a mother, a lover. They had no one in that city – or in any other, really – besides themselves. I could also say they had nothing, but that wouldn't be entirely true.

Besides his guitar, Raul had a rented phone, a record player with FM radio, and a thrush in a birdcage called Carlos Gardel. Saul, a color television with a screen burn-in, sketchbooks, bottles of China ink, and a book of Van Gogh reproductions. In his bedroom at the boarding house, hanging on the wall facing his own bed, another Van Gogh reproduction: the room with the crooked wicker chair, the narrow bed, the hardwood floor. Lying in his bed,

Saul sometimes had the impression that the painting was a mirror that showed his own room almost photographically, with nothing missing but himself. It was in moments like these that he'd draw.

They were handsome too, everyone thought so. The women at the office, married, single, got nervous when they arrived, so tall and confident, said one of the assistants, wide-eyed. Unlike the other men, some of whom were even younger, neither of them had the paunch or the downcast posture of someone who stamps and types eight hours a day.

Tan with a blueish beard, Raul was the more fit of the two, with a deep, low voice, perfect for the bitter boleros he liked so much. They had the same height, the same gait, but Saul looked smaller, frailer, perhaps because of his little curls, shiny and fair, his frightened eyes, faint blue. They looked beautiful together, young women liked to say. Easy to look at. Without realizing it exactly, when they were together they refined their gait even more, and almost glistened, so to speak, the beauty inside one sparking the beauty outside the other, and vice versa. As if there was, between those two, a strange and secret harmony.

3

They'd run into each other, quiet but cordial, by the coffee pot in the break room, sometimes chatting about the weather or some nuisance at work before returning to their desks. From time to time, one would ask the other for a cigarette, and then would say things like, I want to quit so bad but I've never really tried, or I've tried so many times, now I've given up. It took time, all of this. And it would have taken even longer, because being private like this, almost distant, was something they brought from far away. From up north, from down south.

Until one day Saul arrived late, and, replying to some vague what happened, he said that he'd been up all night watching an old movie on TV. Out of politeness, or to fulfill some ritual, or just so he wouldn't feel bad for coming in at almost eleven o'clock, rushed, his face unshaven, Raul held his fingers over the typewriter and asked: what movie? *The Children's Hour*, Saul said softly, Audrey Hepburn, Shirley MacLaine, a very old movie, nobody's seen it. Raul looked at him slowly, carefully, what do you mean nobody's seen it? I've seen it and I like it a lot. Uneasy, he invited Saul out for coffee and, on that very cold morning in June, in that ugly building that looked even more than usual like a police station or a psychiatric hospital, they talked incessantly about the film.

Many other movies would come up in the following days, and so smoothly, as if somehow this was inevitable. Personal stories would also come up, pasts, some dreams, small hopes, and above all complaints. About that office, that life, that knot, they confessed one gray Friday afternoon, tight inside the chest. That weekend, for the first time, they wished secretly, the one in his studio apartment, the other at the boarding house, that Saturday and Sunday would pass swiftly, that the days would quickly turn the corner of midnight to arrive faster on Monday, when they'd finally meet: for coffee. So it was, one saying that he'd had too much to drink, the other that he'd slept almost the entire time. Those two talked about so many things that morning, many things except for the absence they barely knew they felt.

The thoughtful women in the office planned the weekly happy hour at the bars, gafieiras, clubs, parties in somebody's apartment, then in somebody else's. At first reluctant, they eventually gave in, though they'd almost always hide in the corners or on balconies to tell their endless stories. One night, Raul found a guitar and sang *"Tú Me Acostumbraste."* And Saul had too much to drink and puked in the bathroom. On their way to their separate cabs, Raul talked for the first time about how his marriage had come undone. With unsteady steps, Saul told him about his past engagement. And they agreed, drunk, that they were both tired of all the women in the world, their complicated plots, their petty demands. That they preferred this, now, alone, owning their own lives. Even though, and this they didn't say, they didn't know what to do with them.

The next day, hungover, Saul didn't show up at work nor did he call. Restless, Raul spent the day wandering through the cold and deserted halls, softly singing *"Tú Me Acostumbraste"* between countless cups of coffee and half a pack of cigarettes more than he usually smoked.

4

The weekends became so long that one day, in the middle of some conversation, Raul gave Saul his phone number, call if you need something, if you get sick, you never know. On a Sunday afternoon, Saul called just to ask what the other one was doing, and paid him a visit, and they ate dinner together, a very nice home-cooked meal the maid had prepared the previous day. It was then that they spoke, united in their sourness, of the desert, of the souls. They'd known each other for nearly six months. Saul got along with Carlos Gardel, who rehearsed a shy performance at nightfall. But Raul was the one who sang: *"Perfídia," "La Barca,"* and at Saul's request, *"Tú Me Acostumbraste,"* once more, twice. Saul especially liked that little part that went like this, *sutil llegaste a mí como una tentación llenando de inquietud mi corazón.* They played a few games of buraco and, at around nine, Saul left.

On Monday, they didn't say a word about the day before. But they talked more than ever and went to the café many times. The young women around them liked to pry, and sometimes whispered, though the two of them never noticed. That week, they had lunch together for the first time at Saul's boarding house, and he wished he could take Raul up to his room to show him his drawings, visitors weren't allowed at night, but now it was already five to two and the punch clock at work was ruthless. It was around that time that they began to leave and arrive together, usually very happy. Shortly after that, Raul snuck into the boarding house, a bottle of brandy in his coat pocket, *Sandra* as an excuse, which they then watched on Saul's TV. Sitting on the floor, backs against the narrow bed, they could barely pay attention to the movie. They couldn't stop talking. While singing "Io Che Non Vivo," Raul noticed the drawings. Later, looking longingly at the Van Gogh reproduction, he asked how Saul could live in such a small room. He looked genuinely worried. Isn't it sad? he asked. Saul smiled hard: you get used to it.

Now Saul always called on Sundays. And came to see him. They'd have dinner or lunch, drink, smoke, talk the entire time. While Saul sang – sometimes "El Día Que Me Quieras," sometimes "Noche de Ronda" – Saul would slowly caress Carlos Gardel's little head, perched on his index finger. Sometimes they looked at each other. And always smiled. One night, because it was raining, Saul ended up sleeping on the couch. The next day, they arrived together at the office, hair wet from the shower. The young women didn't talk to them. The paunchy and downcast men exchanged a few looks that neither of the two would understand, if they even noticed. But they didn't notice a thing, not the looks, not the few jokes. At ten to six, they left together, tall and confident, to watch the latest Jane Fonda movie.

5

At the beginning of spring, it was Saul's birthday. Because Raul thought his friend was too lonely, or for some other reason like that, Raul gave him the birdcage with Carlos Gardel. Then at the beginning of summer, it was Raul's turn. Because Saul didn't have any money and the walls of his friend's studio were bare, Saul gave him his Van Gogh reproduction. But between those two birthdays, something happened.

Up north, in early December, Raul's mother died and he had to leave town for a week. Disoriented, Saul wandered the halls of the office waiting for a phone call that didn't come, trying to no avail to focus on the dispatches, processes, protocols. At night, in his room, he'd turn on the TV and pass the time with cheap soap operas or draw eyes that grew bigger and bigger, while caressing Carlos Gardel. He drank a lot that week. And had a dream: he was walking among his colleagues, all in black, reproachful. Except for Raul, all in white, waiting for him with open arms. Then, holding each other tight, so close that each could smell the other. Saul woke up thinking he should be the one grieving.

Raul came back griefless. On a Friday afternoon, he called the office to ask Saul to come see him. His deep, low voice sounded even lower, deeper. Saul went. Raul's beard had grown. Strangely, he didn't look older or harsher but instead had the face of a boy. They had too much to drink that night. Raul talked about his mother for a long time, I could have been nicer to her, he said, and didn't sing. When Saul was about to leave, Raul started to cry. Before he knew what he was doing, Saul stretched out his hand, and only then realized his fingers had touched Raul's unshaven face. With no time to understand it, they held each other tight. And so close each could smell the other: Raul, wilted flower, musty drawer; Saul, aftershave balm, talcum powder. A long time passed. Saul's hand touching Raul's beard, Raul's fingers in Saul's little curls. No words. In the silence, they could hear a faucet dripping in the distance. So much time passed that when Saul finally reached for the ashtray, his cigarette was just a long stick of ash which he crushed without realizing.

They stepped away from each other, then. Raul said something like I have nobody else in the world, and Saul said something else like, you have me now, and forever. They used big words – nobody, world, forever – and held both hands at once, looking into each other's eyes, full of smoke and alcohol. Even though it was Friday and they didn't have work in the morning, Saul said good night. He walked for hours through the deserted streets, no one around but cats and hookers. At home, he caressed Carlos Gardel until they fell asleep. But before that, not knowing why, he broke down crying, feeling alone and poor and ugly and unfortunate and confused and abandoned and drunk and sad, sad, sad. He thought of calling Raul, but he didn't have any quarters and it was late.

6

Christmas arrived, then they spent New Year's Eve together, declining their colleagues' invitations. Raul gave Saul a reproduction of "The Birth of Venus," and he put it up on the wall precisely where Van Gogh's room had been. Saul gave Raul the *Greatest Hits of Dalva de Oliveira*. They listened to "Nossas Vidas" over and over, paying close attention to the part that said something like even our kisses feel like the kisses of those who've never loved.

It was on the night of the thirty-first, champagne already open in Raul's apartment, when Saul raised his glass and toasted, to our friendship, which will never ever end. They drank until near-collapse. Before going to bed, while changing clothes in the bathroom, very drunk, Saul said he was going to sleep naked. Raul looked at him and said, Your body is beautiful. So is yours, said Saul, and lowered his eyes. They both lay naked, one on the bed behind the dresser, the other on the couch. The entire night, one could see the blazing cherry of the other's cigarette, piercing the darkness like a demon's burning eye. In the morning, Saul left without a word. Raul wouldn't notice the deep circles under his eyes.

When January came around, it was almost time to go on vacation – and they'd planned, together, perhaps Parati, Ouro Preto, Porto Seguro. They were surprised one morning when their boss called them into his office, right before noon. It was very hot. The boss, sweaty, got straight to the point. He'd received some anonymous letters. He refused to show them. Pale, they listened to phrases like "unusual and obtrusive relationship," "shameless aberration," "insalubrious behavior," "mental defect," always signed by An Attentive Guardian of Morals. Saul lowered his pale eyes, but Raul stood up. He looked even taller with one hand on his friend's shoulder and the other boldly raised in the air. He still managed to say the word *never*, before the boss, inserted among comments like our-office's-reputation, said coldly: You two are fired.

They slowly emptied each of their drawers, the room deserted at lunchtime, without exchanging a glance. It was summer. The sun burned the metal tables. Raul put into a big brown envelope two huge eyes, no irises or pupils, a gift from Saul, who put into his own big brown envelope, with coffee stains, the lyrics to *"Tú Me Acostumbraste,"* handwritten by Raul on an August afternoon. They took the elevator together, in silence.

But when they walked out the door of that big, old building, as dull as a hospital or a police station, their colleagues observing them from a window up above, one in a white shirt, the other in blue, they were even taller and more confident. They stood for a few minutes before the building. Then they hailed a cab together, Raul opening the door for Saul. Ai ai, someone yelled from the window. But they didn't hear it. The cab had already turned the corner.

For the rest of that month, on dusty afternoons, when the sun looked like a giant yolk in the cloudless sky, no one managed to get any work done at the office. Nearly all of them had the distinct feeling they would live unhappily ever after. And they did.

Moldy Strawberries

For José Márcio Penido

Let me take you down
'Cause I'm going to Strawberry Fields
Nothing is real
And nothing to get hung about
Strawberry Fields forever
—Lennon & McCartney, "Strawberry Fields Forever"

PRELUDE

However (he now said things like *however*) he was there and this was how he saw himself. It was inside this that he had to move, under the risk of. Not surviving, for example – and did he want to? He listed phrases like that's-how-things-go or what-can-one-do-what-can-one-do or simply but-what-matters-after-all. And each day that taste of moldy strawberries spread in his mouth, sickly green, kept for a long time in the bottom of some drawer.

ALLEGRO AGITATO

So you're in excellent shape, the doctor's elegant voice, grizzly temples, wearing beige, *ton sur ton*, from the polished shoes to the loose tie, a nice balance between untidy and laid-back. There's nothing wrong with your heart or your body, much less your brain. Sir. He lit another cigarette, one of those you smoke twice as much because it has half the poison, but it's not in the brain where I have cancer, doctor, it's in the soul, and this won't show up in any check-up.

The disease of our time, I know, I know, now he'll start spinning his social-political-psychoanalytic considerations about the Alarming Rise of Hypochondria Motivated by the Paranoia of Large Urban Centers, his face well-shaven, his mouth with perfect dentures, a hooker once said that doctors are the biggest perverts (perhaps because of the constant intimacy with human flesh?), and this one? Quick, he analyzed: sucks pussy at the most, practices-oral-sex, he'd call it, meticulously brushing his dentures after, naturally if you can reduce the smoking that's always good, a lot of milk, boiled, of course, to avoid pathogens, fresh air, a bit of exercise, jogging, perhaps, thinking more about the future than the more immediate term, of course. But what if the future, doctor, is inevitable, finally someone pressing the button and the metallic mushroom ripping out our raw flesh? he carefully tapped his cigarette on the ashtray, a metal ashtray, he hated anything made of metal, and everything in that doctor's office was chromed, Formica, acrylic, antiseptic, un-con-tam-i-nat-ed, much like the doctor himself, never daring beyond the beige. On the wall, the still life with dry white grapes, pale pears, ashen apples. No gaping watermelons, no ripe pitangas, no bleeding strawberries. A moldy strawberry – and this taste, doctor, always in my mouth?

Heartburn, indigestion, his obliging smile, at least thirty percent real teeth (what to do, after all? dance an Argentine tango, or sing it? he hummed quietly *quiero emborrachar mi corazón para olvidar un loco amor que más que amor fue una traición*, he had verses he could use, suitable for any occasion, this secret advantage over everyone else, but so secret that it was also a disadvantage, you know? neither do I, pop-up verses of our finest poetry, Argentine tangos & frenzy rocks, an emphasis on guitar solos). A mild-mild sedative, just five milligrams, for you to take three times a day, upon waking, after lunch, at bedtime, glazed eyes, quiet mind, still heart, systole, pause, diastole, pause, systole, pause, diastole, no pointless tachycardia. Chemical brakes on the emotions. That's how he'd go on to move around, lighthearted with Double O Seven briefcases, Cardin jackets, Fiorucci labels, mildly drugged up, demons sufficiently numbed so as not to bother anyone. Feelings forbidden, feelings walking around, desperate feelings walking upside down, warm feelings forbidden, frivolous anxieties, morbid fantasies, and useless memories, a Bayer nirvana if it's even Bayer. He sighed, he sighed a lot lately, picked up the prescription, signed a good check, and left before hearing the gentle because anyhow, you're still so young.

ADAGIO SOSTENUTO

When he woke up, the sunlight wasn't falling on the patio anymore, which simply meant it was sometime-after-two-o'-clock. He had taken three pills, one for the morning, one for lunchtime, one for bedtime, but all at once – and the taste remained in his mouth. Strawberry, he thought, and he wanted, then, like in the old days, to listen to the Beatles again, but still lying in bed he didn't feel like taking the two steps to the record player, and whatever happened to them, lost among all the Simones and Donna Summers, so very long ago, he didn't even like pot anymore. He fondled his limp dick, with faint interest, wishing to interrupt that silence so typical of empty apartments, the maid wouldn't come, he hadn't put any gas in the car yet, or cashed his check, or found a quick fuck for himself, or taken any of the after-lunch-on-Friday-precautions, and he had to. He had to invent a whole day, or two, because tomorrow is Sunday, and Monday who knows what will happen.

He lit another cigarette, fasting and thinking of ulcers, emphysemas, cirrhosis, fibrous layers covering the liver, but does the liver continue to exist underneath the fibers or is it consumed by them? No one would know how to explain, synthetic underwear, those that cause pruritus & impotence, some cash tossed onto the rug, perfect Persian imitation. The phone rang, as it sometimes did at this hour, stopping at the comma before the blank page, he stretched out his arm, beautiful fingers he had, knotty in the joints, which shows sensibility & anxiety, Alice would say, but Alice had left a long time ago, that bitch I actually ate pretty well, arousing her clitoris, *comme il faut*, this is not how it's said how it's done how it's. The phone rang one more time, one more time then another and another still, while with one hand he turned on the radio, releasing a disheveled violin sound, Wagner, he presumed, who had his culture, his books, valkyries, Nazisms, Dachaus, Jews, while with the other hand he fondled his dick now starting to throb, aroused perhaps by the violins, the Jews, the Davids.

The phone stopped ringing, the phone didn't make any special sound when it stopped ringing, it should gasp, moan when penetrated, hard and hot, fucking Jew, must be involved with that kibbutz in the middle of that sand, growing wheat, not wheat, it's too dry, olives perhaps, the warm head of his dick throbbing in his palm, this is what he got for trading Albert Camus for Anna Seghers, Pervitin for codeine, horniness is only resolved in bed, not by lending someone a book or introducing someone to a new drug, take note, learn, but now it's *troppo* late, everything is in the past, my life is an unresolved yesterday, it's good like this. And idiotic.

He suddenly stood up. That was when the nausea took over, he only had enough time to walk to the bathroom and puke in between panting and growling, where are you all hiding right now, for fuck's sake, where are the rural communities, the nirvanas with no tolls, the acid in every water tank of every city, the blue of the tiles starting to glisten, Maya, Samara, who sometimes came back. Suddenly lysergic in the middle of a dizzy sentence, of an insufficient gesture, of a filthy act like this one, puking the entire mild-mild fifteen milligrams. Alice opened her thighs where the fur thickened into red hair, then moaned real nice, warm moisture inside. Burned-out neurons, still a certain number to spare, then slowly they die out, won't be restored ever again, how many do I still have left, god, and David's hand covered in dark hair feeling my veins until they swelled up, almost obscene, throbbing light blue, you know, man, when I shoot you up like this sometimes I even think that. Sleepless nights and sunshine casting a green light on our pale faces, and our skin so dry, and our voices hoarse from all the talking and smoking and smoking and talking. He puked some more. Disgust, *saudade*. I'm a successful ad-man, smooth, swirling in the clouds, Carvalho said that swirling-in-the-clouds is the shit, what a find, man, while I looked at him and didn't say anything like I myself have swirled in the clouds once before, and now I'm here, bogged down in this colorful shit, fucked up & well paid.

Strawberry fields: mixed in the puke, he could distinguish here and there pieces of strawberry floating in the water, greenish with mold.

ANDANTE OSTINATO

Neither yesterday nor tomorrow, there's only the now, Jack Nicholson repeated before getting beaten to death, while he glanced at David lying at the bottom of the well, so deep he'd need a ladder to get down there, sidestepping the rubble of the little town that was both Köln after the war and Passo da Guanxuma at the same time, with that lake in the middle where boats kept departing and arriving, he'd never know, and it doesn't matter, Alice ran between the cypresses at the cemetery without gravestones while he yelled, Alice, Alice, my daughter, when are you going to convince yourself that you aren't on the other side of the mirror anymore, until he found Billie Holiday standing by the ladder, between demolished walls, the steps going up into nothing, hovering in space, repeating *You've changed, baby oh baby, you've changed*, she offered her hand to help John Lennon, but when she opened her bloody mouth that awful smell of rotten strawberries came out like wind coming out of a box, like wind coming from the sea, a former sea, a sea almost infinite where not a drop is past, not a drop is future, everything is motionless present and in continuous action, the smell of sea air like the breath of the bionic golden panther. So many years of Freudian Kleinian Jungian Reichian Rankian Rogerian Gestaltian analysis. And strawberry mold.

Screams. But he woke up with the electronic beep before he even opened his mouth. The fresh night air lulled the white curtains, like sails from a stranded boat, a ship with billowing sails? there's no use in crying, Alice, I've already said this is madness, stop cutting those damn lines, your nose will end up getting a third hole, it's better to be a Buddhist monk in Vitória do Espírito Santo or a Carmelite barefoot in Calcutta or the most puta of the putas in the putaquepariu, don't look at me like that from the bottom of the well, don't bug me with this hypnotic beep, I'm here, my darling, in the rubble.

He turned off the television, walked out onto the patio filled with dusty plants, I should take better care of them, if it weren't for the living presence inside me, deteriorating, being eaten away, the cell going crazy in my soul fermenting the disgusting taste on my tongue. The smell of that single jasmine spreading over seven overpasses on the main avenue. A light push was enough, bent over the railing, stiff, dead from the waist down, from the waist up, from the waist out, from the waist in – what difference does it make?

Let's officialize what's already happened: I lost a piece of myself, a while back. I didn't even die from it.

MINUET AND RONDO

Daylight dawned. There was no one in the streets.

No, it went like this: bending over the railing, first he looked up – and saw that the blue of the sky was nearly black with some parts going gray, lighter and lighter toward the horizon, if there was a horizon, anyway behind the last buildings that were, say, he considered, a surrogate for the horizon. And daylight dawned, he then concluded. Bending over the railing, he looked down – and saw no activity in the long street, no cars, no people, only the seven overpasses also deserted. There was no one in the streets, he then concluded.

Bending over the railing, daylight dawned.

At the same time, immediately after, one person from-inside-him thought: what if someone really finally pressed the button? and what if that gray in the surrogate for the horizon was the metallic light? and I was asleep when all this happened? and now I'm alone in the city, in the country, on the continent, on the planet? He knew he wasn't. And another person from-inside-him also thought, going further, clearer, almost organized, not fully though because to be honest this wasn't really a thought or an emotion, but something more like that natural gray light welling up over the horizon, if there was a horizon, or like the fresh air blowing the curtains, or as if a wave had arisen from that motionless sea, active in that place where the light begins, where the wind begins, where the wave begins, from this place I don't know, neither do you, neither does he right now: something sprouted like, sorry, a light, a wind, a wave. Exactly: a wave, calm or gasping for air, a wind, minuano or sirocco, a light, morbid or bright, I repeated that it sprouted, he repeated in disbelief.

He was sure. Or had clear suspicions. That there was no harm, in the sense of loss, but accumulations in the sense of gaining? Yes, yes. Transmutations? No irreversible losses, alices-davids gone with the wind, but rather auspicious replacements, as if they were magical, they would come in their own time, what time would alices-davids bring? It wasn't a chemical sensation. His mouth wasn't dry and his heart wasn't racing and his pupils weren't dilated. He sat there exactly as he was, no additives.

I'm leaving, he thought. The road is long.

He then touched his own body. An inner glory: that's how he baptized it, solemn, infinitely delicate, when it bloomed. The harp, that was what came to him, ridiculous complacent, cor-nu-co-pi-a, he spelled out, I want a baroque moment like this, he wished. But dressed in yellow as he was, against the sky, seen from the back, imagining there was a film camera placed here by the door framing him right now, looking almost byzantine, gold over blue, mystical meagerness, with his culture, his books. And not a trace of guilt. Gothic, he moaned, twisted, brought his hands together with his sex, his belly, his chest, his face, and raised his arms above his head.

The sun was rising.

Maybe he would be admitted to a hospital any minute now, but really he felt as if he could hear the opening notes to *Le Sacre du Printemps*. The moldy taste of strawberries had disappeared. Like a headache, sudden. He was five years older than thirty. He was halfway there, if seventy was his number. But he was a newborn man when he slowly turned around, turned around on his own feet one hundred and eighty degrees, to go and slip through the barrier of the overpass, until he could kneel down on the dark tiles, his hands covering his sex. He opened his hands. Absolutely calm, absolutely clear, absolutely alone while he considered, carefully, observing the flowerbeds down below: would it be possible to grow strawberries here? And if not, to find someplace somewhere else? Fresh red strawberries.

He thought maybe yes.

Maybe yes.

Yes.

Translator's Acknowledgements

This book has been generously supported by a PEN/Heim Translation Fund Grant. "Beyond the Point" was first published in *The Massachusetts Review*, "Passing through a Great Sorrow" in *The Kenyon Review*, "Fat Tuesday" was excerpted in Two Lines' *Cuíer*, "The Day Uranus Entered Scorpio (Old Story with Benefits)" appeared in *BOMB*, and "Those Two" appeared in *The American Scholar*.